AN ANTHOLOGY OF

Butterflies

AND Moths

WARNING: This book is an introduction to the amazing world of butterflies and moths and is for general-information purposes only. We would not encourage butterfly or moth collection, unless done carefully and for scientific identification. Insect populations are generally declining, and several butterflies and moths are protected by law. Some moths can also become house pests, others have irritating scales that can cause skin irritation or respiratory problems in some people.

AN ANTHOLOGY OF

Butterflies
AND Moths

Written by Richard Jones
Illustrated by Angela Rizza
and Daniel Long

Contents

What are butterflies and moths?

Butterflies and moths come in a huge range of different shapes, colors, and patterns.

Butterflies and moths are insects—they are actually very similar to one another and can be difficult to tell apart. There are about 180,000 different known types of butterfly and moth in the world, but many unknown species probably remain undiscovered, especially deep in tropical jungles.

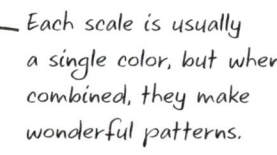

The oleander hawk moth has a beautiful swirling pattern of greens and pinks.

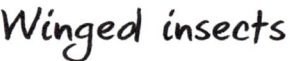

Winged insects

Butterflies and moths belong to the insect order Lepidoptera, which means "scaled wing." This is because the four large, broad wings are covered with tiny overlapping colored scales.

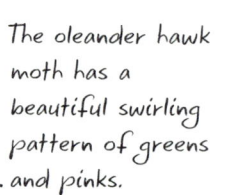

Each scale is usually a single color, but when combined, they make wonderful patterns.

Colorful scales

The flat scales combine together to form many different colors and patterns—like the small pieces of an art mosaic. The scales have developed, or evolved, from simple hairs, which over time became flattened and ribbed.

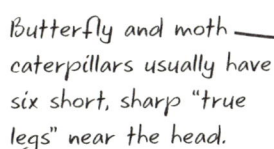

Butterfly and moth caterpillars usually have six short, sharp "true legs" near the head.

Caterpillars

Butterflies and moths develop from caterpillars, which look nothing like the adult winged insects that they will become. Caterpillars are often secretive—being very good at hiding away from predators. Once they develop into adults, they have wings to fly off to find mates and start new colonies.

There are usually 10 (sometimes up to 16) soft, fleshy "prolegs" toward the tail end.

Butterflies in mythology

Because of their bright colors and natural beauty, butterflies have been admired and studied for thousands of years. In Greek mythology, Psyche, goddess of the soul, was usually represented as a woman with butterfly wings.

Spot the difference!

Many people ask, "What is the difference between a butterfly and a moth?" The answer is "not much!" The traditional thinking is that butterflies have broad wings and are brightly colored, while moths have narrower wings and are generally a dull brown. However, butterflies are just one group alongside a huge range of different moth types—all belonging to the insect order called Lepidoptera. There are plenty of brightly colored, day-flying moths, and many small, drab, brown butterflies.

Bright colors often help a butterfly identify a mate of the same species.

Butterflies

Generally, butterfly species are those with large, broad wings that they spread wide when basking in the sun, or fold together like a book when resting, or roosting. They often have bright colors, fly during the daytime, and their antennae are long, usually swollen into a club at the tip. Butterflies include many of the familiar insects we see flying in our parks and gardens on warm, sunny days.

Although they are small and brown and hold their wings at different angles, skippers are still classified as butterflies.

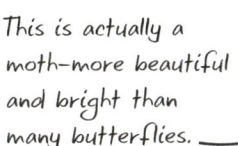

Why is a butterfly so called?

No one knows how the word butterfly originated. It may be from the bright yellow, butter-colored brimstone, which is one of the first butterflies to be seen flying around in early spring in northern Europe.

Brimstone butterfly

This is actually a moth—more beautiful and bright than many butterflies.

This day-flying moth has clubbed antennae like many butterflies.

Moths

The insects we usually call moths fly at night and have small, narrow wings that they fold tentlike over the body. Moths mostly have dull-brown, mottled, or camouflaged patterns and narrow or feathery antennae. People often imagine these as vague, shadowy shapes swooping around streetlights, or tiny brown things flying out of the clothes closet.

Caterpillars

Just as butterflies and moths are really the same thing, there is also no easy way to tell butterfly caterpillars from moth caterpillars. They both vary from brightly colored to dull green or brown, smooth to bristly, long and thin to short and fat.

Feeding time

While butterflies and moths do feed, caterpillars do most of the eating and all of the growing! Almost all caterpillars enjoy munching on plants, whereas most butterflies and moths feed on nectar from flowers.

How caterpillars feed

Different species eat different types of plant, often just one part, such as the buds, flowers, leaves, stems, roots, fruits, seeds, bark, or fallen leaves. From hatching from the egg to being fully grown, a caterpillar will eat hundreds or thousands of times its own weight in food.

Two large chewing jaws help grind up tough plant material.

Some caterpillars can cut holes and rupture stems, blocking off the supply of nutrients and water throughout the plant.

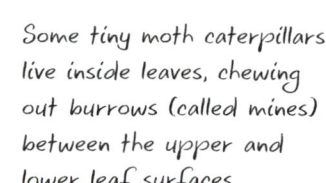

Some tiny moth caterpillars live inside leaves, chewing out burrows (called mines) between the upper and lower leaf surfaces.

How butterflies and moths feed

Instead of chewing jaws, butterflies and moths have a long, narrow, tubular tongue, called a proboscis. This is used to drink nectar from flowers, water from wet mud, or oozing sap from damaged tree bark. When they are no longer growing, the insects feed on the sugary chemicals to get the energy to fly, mate, and lay eggs.

Made up of two tubes, the tongue is usually kept curled up when the insect is not feeding.

At the time of feeding, the two tubes zip together in the middle—and it is through this that the liquid meal is drunk.

Butterflies often drink liquid from strange places, such as animal droppings and rotting fruit. They also get nutrients as well as liquid from these sources.

Metamorphosis

When a caterpillar is fully grown, it undergoes a wonderful transformation. After the final soft caterpillar skin is molted, a hard, shell-like skin forms—the chrysalis. The inside of the caterpillar now turns into a semiliquid mass of nutrients to form the adult butterfly or moth.

Caterpillar versus butterfly

Adult butterflies and moths have many features not found in caterpillars—antennae, wings, large complex eyes, sucking mouthparts, segmented legs, and male and female reproductive organs that produce sperm or eggs. In a caterpillar, the beginnings of these structures are present, but only as tiny groups of embryo cells. These features are prevented from developing in the caterpillar by a special chemical called a juvenile hormone.

When the caterpillar reaches its full-grown size, the juvenile hormone is turned off.

1

2

The final caterpillar skin is molted and the chrysalis is revealed.

It can take from a few days to many months for the adult to emerge from the chrysalis.

Chrysalis opens

When the adult insect inside is ready, it splits open the chrysalis and crawls out. At first, its wings are soft and wrinkled—it needs to expand these and dry off before it can fly.

5

4

3

The adult crawls out of the chrysalis. It now has to pump liquid into the wing veins to make them expand—ready for flight.

Inside the hard chrysalis, the adult's legs, antennae, wings, and eyes start to develop.

13

Tropical rainforests

Tropical rainforests are home to more species of butterfly and moth than anywhere else on Earth. Much of the diversity is high up in the tree canopy, where caterpillars feed on the very many different types of tropical trees, vines, and creepers. Adult butterflies fly in the sunshine, only occasionally venturing down to the dark forest floor. Moths mostly hide during the day, resting in leaves or on tree trunks, but fly at night. While it may be easy to spot these insects due to their large size and bright colors, new and different butterflies and moths are still being discovered deep in the jungle. However, the trees are valued for their lumber and are often cut down across huge areas.

Glasswing

Greta oto

True to their name, glasswings look as if they are made of glass. The butterflies flutter slowly through dark forests and are difficult to see unless they rest on a leaf or flower. There are scales on their wings, but these are so small and narrow that they look like microscopic hairs. This, together with the fact that they are thinly spread, makes the wings appear transparent.

The colored scales are only in narrow margins.

It has just four walking legs.

15

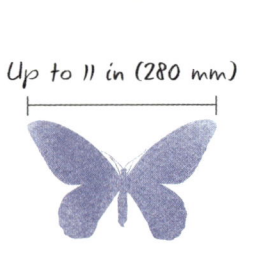

Up to 11 in (280 mm)

Queen Alexandra's birdwing

Ornithoptera alexandrae

The female of this species, with a wingspan of up to 11 in (280 mm), is the largest butterfly in the world. The smaller and more brightly colored male looks completely different. This butterfly was first found in 1906 and was named in honor of Queen Alexandra of Denmark.

It has long, narrow wings that allow strong, fast flight.

The male has streaks of metallic-green scales.

The female is dark brown with cream patches.

The upper part of the forewing is dark brown.

Up to 7.4 in (190 mm)

Only the male has the rich, gold metallic bands on its wings.

Wallace's golden birdwing

Ornithoptera croesus

In 1859, English traveler and scientist Alfred Russel Wallace first saw this beautiful butterfly high up in the jungle trees of Bacan, a tropical island in Indonesia. He was so excited by what he'd seen that he had a headache for the rest of the day! Wallace named the butterfly after Croesus, king of Lydia (now Türkiye). This ancient king ruled about 2,500 years ago and was famed for his gold.

Notes

· Only known to live on a few islands in Indonesia

· Female is dark brown with white markings

· At risk due to deforestation and overuse of chemicals used to kill insects that damage crops

Up to 4.7 in (120 mm)

The forewing tips have two small white marks.

The blue color changes as the insect flies, catching the sunlight at different angles.

Blue morpho

Morpho menelaus

B lue morpho butterflies are among the most beautiful insects in the world. They fly high through the tops of rainforest trees. In fact, the blue is not a true color, but is caused by tiny grooves on the scales that break and scatter white sunlight, reflecting blue wavelengths. These grooves are only made visible by the most powerful microscopes.

Notes

· Lives throughout Central and South America

· Females have broad black edges on the wings

· Metallic-blue wings were sometimes used to make expensive jewelry

Owl butterfly

Caligo idomeneus

Up to 7 in (180 mm)

When this large butterfly rests with its wings closed together, the underside eyespots make it look like the head of an owl. Also, the wavy, white-and-brown lines resemble fluffy feathers. This clever trick is called mimicry, and it will make any predator hesitate before trying to attack, giving the butterfly a few extra moments to escape.

Streaked wing patterns look like bird feathers

The curve of white dots makes the eye pattern look moist and domed.

The sleek caterpillar of the owl butterfly feeds on banana leaves.

Indian leaf butterfly

Kallima inachus

When this butterfly flies through the forest, the bar of color on the upper surface of the wings seems to flash on and off like a beacon. However, when the butterfly lands to rest on a twig or stem, it closes its wings and only the perfectly camouflaged underside is shown. As a result, any predator chasing the on-and-off orange marking is confused by this disappearing act.

The wing tip is drawn out to a slightly curved point.

Notes

• Lives in India, Pakistan, China, Japan, and parts of Southeast Asia

• Wet-season forms of this butterfly are darker and look like damp leaves

It has a dried-leaf pattern on its wings.

The small kidney-shaped mark on the front wing looks like a leaf blemish.

Up to 5.9 in (150 mm)

The tip of the wing juts out and looks like a leaf-tip point.

Borneo leafwing

Phyllodes verhuelli

This moth hides by looking just like a leaf when it rests with its wings closed. To frighten off predators, the moth flicks open its wings to reveal a red-and-white flash. This can startle a predator, giving the moth a vital few moments to make its escape.

With a flick of the moth's wings, a red flash startles a predator.

Up to 1.8 in (45 mm)

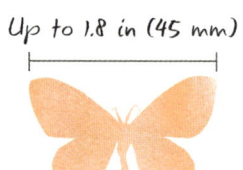

Eighty-eight butterfly

Diaethria clymena

The upper surface of the wings of the eighty-eight butterfly is black, but with a dash of metallic-blue or greenish scales. In contrast, the underside is brightly patterned with red, white, and black. When this stunning-looking insect flies it seems to flick on and off through the air like a light.

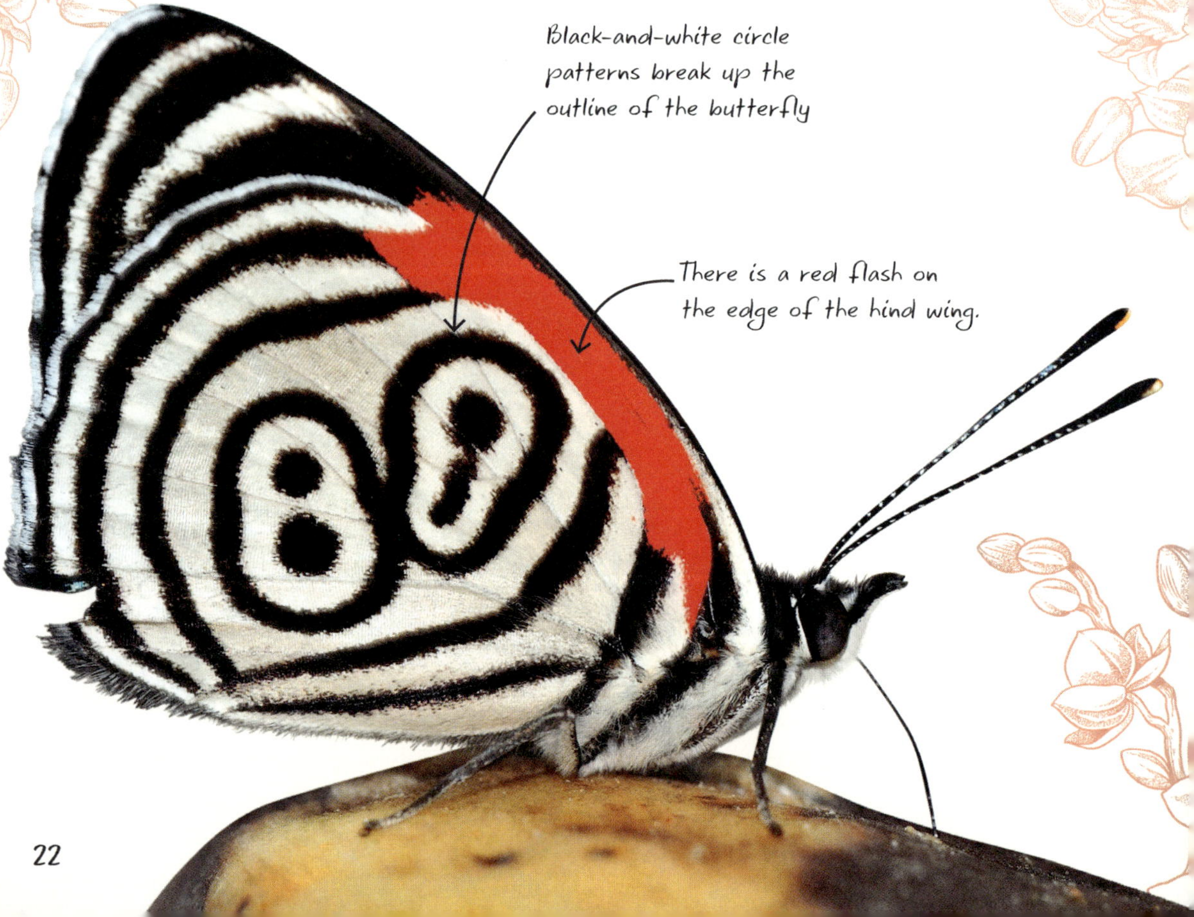
Black-and-white circle patterns break up the outline of the butterfly
There is a red flash on the edge of the hind wing.

Small, black streaks look like the fly's legs

The irregular outline of the orange patch resembles a splash of liquid.

Bird-dropping and flies moth

Macrocilix maia

When it rests on a large leaf, this moth's wing pattern looks like two small red-eyed blue bottle flies feeding on bird droppings. It does not look like a tasty mouthful for a predator, and this may help the moth to avoid being eaten by birds.

Notes

• Caterpillars feed on the leaves of Chinese cork oak trees

• Lives in India, Japan, China, Korea, and other parts of East and Southeast Asia

Up to 11.8 in (300 mm)

Atlas moth

Attacus atlas

Curved wing tips resemble a lizard or snake head

This giant moth is well named—in Greek mythology, Atlas was the giant who held up the skies. The species has the largest wings of any moth, although the white witch moth has the widest wings. When the Atlas moth is resting among leaves, its curved wing tips, with their dark spots and red streaks, look like the head of a lizard or snake.

The male has very feathery antennae.

This moth has clear, triangular patches on its wings.

Notes

• Lives in India, China, and Southeast Asia

• Spiny caterpillars feed on the leaves of citrus, cinnamon, and guava trees

Up to 4.7 in (120 mm)

The dark edge of the wings helps it blend into the tree branch.

The brown color in the middle of the tail separates the tips from the main wings.

African moon moth

Argema mimosae

When this moth rests on a tree branch, its wings rest together to form a leaflike, half-moon shape. The long tails look as if they are separate from the main wings. This may distract or confuse a predator so that it strikes the flat tips, which move around gently as the moth rests on a leaf or tree branch.

Up to 11.8 in (300 mm)

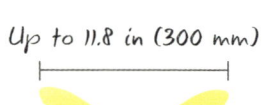

White witch moth

Thysania agrippina

This moth gets its name from stories that arose around it in the 19th century. Early hunters tried to shoot it down from high in the treetops with guns that fired out a cloud of tiny lead pellets. The pellets may have made small holes in the moth's large wings, but often missed its slim body, so the moth kept flying, like a magically protected witch.

The zigzag streaks on the wings help the moth blend into lichen-covered tree trunks.

Notes

• Has the greatest wingspan of any moth in the world

• Found in South and Central America, but sometimes individuals migrate into the southern United States

Up to 6.2 in (160 mm)

Long, narrow wings allow the moth to hover in midair as it inserts its tongue into the long, thin flower.

The tongue is the longest of any known moth.

Darwin's orchid has long, whiplike nectary tubes.

Morgan's sphinx moth

Xanthopan morganii

The tongue of this moth can reach more than 11 in (280 mm) when uncurled. The moth uses it to reach deep into the flowers of a particular species of orchid known as Darwin's orchid, where the nectar is stored at the end of a thin tube that is more than 11.8 in (300 mm).

Up to 2 in (50 mm)

Green dragontail
Lamproptera meges

This butterfly often visits mud at the edges of streams to drink water. Its long tails wave up and down slightly, similar to a grasshopper's antennae. This can confuse a predator, which may not be able to figure out which is the head end of the butterfly, and so fail in its attempt to sneak around the back to pounce.

Notes

- Length 2.3 in (60 mm) to the tip of the tail

- Lives in India, China, and Southeast Asia

The front wings are clear, but edged with a black bar, adding to the illusion that they might be the back legs of a grasshopper!

White-tipped tails

The wings are mostly shining blue but with a band of reddish spots.

Up to 2.6 in (65 mm)

Wet-season summer form, which is mostly orange

Gaudy commodore

Precis octavia

During the drier, winter period, specimens of this butterfly are mostly blue, with a band of reddish spots along the wings. However, adults that hatch from the chrysalis in the wet summer are bright orange with black markings, and these are smaller. Originally, the two were thought to be completely different butterfly species. Rare intermediates—which display markings from both types—can occur between the seasons.

Up to 4 in (105 mm)

Long, trailing
featherlike tails

Mocker swallowtail

Papilio dardanus

The mocker swallowtail is one of the largest butterflies in Africa. Just as swallows have long, trailing tail feathers, so does the mocker swallowtail butterfly. The males of this species all have the same pale-yellow-and-black color patterns and wingtails. The females, however, vary in coloring and patterning. These range from black, orange, and white to pale pink or blue and black. There is even a female with malelike colors and similar wingtails.

Females copy the patterns of other butterflies, mostly monarchs, to trick predators into thinking they too taste horrible.

African giant swallowtail

Papilio antimachus

The African giant swallowtail is one of the largest butterflies in Africa. It is very rare and only occurs deep in rainforests that are often inaccessible to humans. The males have longer wings than the females, and they sometimes fly down to drink in wet mud. The females, however, prefer to stay high up in the treetops and are rarely seen. Nobody knows what the caterpillar looks like, or what it feeds on.

Up to 9 in (230 mm)

Notes

• Lives in tropical regions of Africa

• Butterflies feed on wet mud water, and they also get nutrients from animal urine and dung

This butterfly's antennae are relatively small for its size.

The black-and-orange pattern is a warning that the butterfly is poisonous.

Up to 0.3 in (7 mm)

Ant-mimic moth

Xestocasis iostrota

When this moth rests on a leaf it looks like a
stinging ant. The moth holds its tufted back legs
in the air to resemble the ant's antennae, and its narrow
wings are broadened and rounded at the tips to mimic
an ant's large head. And to complete the trick, it then
runs around backward on leaves!

Wings have
rounded edges

Rear legs are held
up in the air to
look like antennae

Swollen and
rounded wing
tips look like
large ant eyes

Notes

· Found in India, Japan, Southeast Asia, and northern Australia

· Caterpillars feed on many different plants, including pomegranate trees

· When resting with the wings together, the streaked pattern blends into leaves and twigs

Only the male has these inflatable growths, called coremata

Hair-pencil moth

Creatonotos gangis

This small, streaked moth looks very ordinary when settled, but the male has a peculiar feathery tail, which it can pump up with body fluids when it needs to find a female to mate with. The fine, feathery growths give off a special chemical, called a pheromone. The female senses this scent with her antennae, and she flies toward the source until the moths meet up.

Up to 4.7 in (120 mm)

Verdant hawk moth

Euchloron megaera

This moth is very unusual because although green is a common color in caterpillars, it rarely occurs in the adult stage. When the moth rests, with its wings closed together over its body, it exactly matches the color of leaves. But if it is disturbed, it will flick open its back wings, showing a bright flash of yellow, which can surprise a predator.

Small brown patches look like bits of dead leaf, further helping with the disguise.

Along with the flash of yellow, it also has patches of grayish scales.

It has a striking metallic, grayish-blue pattern.

The bold markings break up the solid outline of the moth, helping it to blend into its surroundings.

Hieroglyphic moth

Diphthera festiva

The pattern of blue-gray marks on the cream background of this moth looks like it has been drawn on in ink—like hieroglyphs drawn onto ancient Egyptian papyrus. Then, when the moth rests with its wings folded over its body, the marks break up the silhouette outline, making it more difficult for birds and other predators to find and eat it. The strong pattern is also a useful warning that the moth is foul-tasting because it contains poison.

Up to 4.3 in (110 mm)

Streaks of metallic-green scales

The caterpillar is black and white and looks like a bird dropping.

Sunset-orange-and-red spot

Madagascan sunset moth
Chrysiridia rhipheus

This day-flying moth is more brightly colored than many butterflies. Indeed, when it was first discovered in 1773, it was described as a butterfly. It took another 50 years for people to realize it was actually a moth! A similar, brightly colored moth called Sloane's Urania used to be found in Jamaica, but, sadly, it became extinct more than 100 years ago because of habitat destruction.

Notes

· The hitchhiking behavior of the sloth moth is called phoresy

· Up to 120 moths have been found living in the fur of a single sloth

· This moth lives in Central and South America

The streaks on the moth's wings blend in with the coarse fur of the sloth.

Sloth moth

Cryptoses choloepi

This small, streaked moth lives in the fur of slow-moving, tree-dwelling mammals called sloths. However, the moth does them no harm. When the sloth climbs down to the forest floor to relieve itself, the female moths fly out and lay their eggs in the sloth's droppings. The caterpillars then feed on the dung. When the adult moths hatch, they fly up into the trees to find another sloth on which to hitch a ride.

The smooth, narrow outline of the moth allows it to push down into the sloth's fur.

Up to 3 in (80 mm)

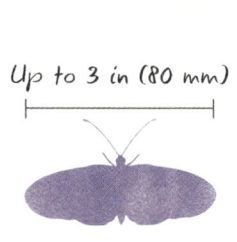

Small postman

Heliconius erato

This butterfly comes in many different color patterns, from black and red, to black and white, to black, white, and red. These patterns vary depending on where in the world the butterfly lives. The small postman flies close to the ground around the edges of the forest, and the butterflies gather in groups to roost in tree branches at night.

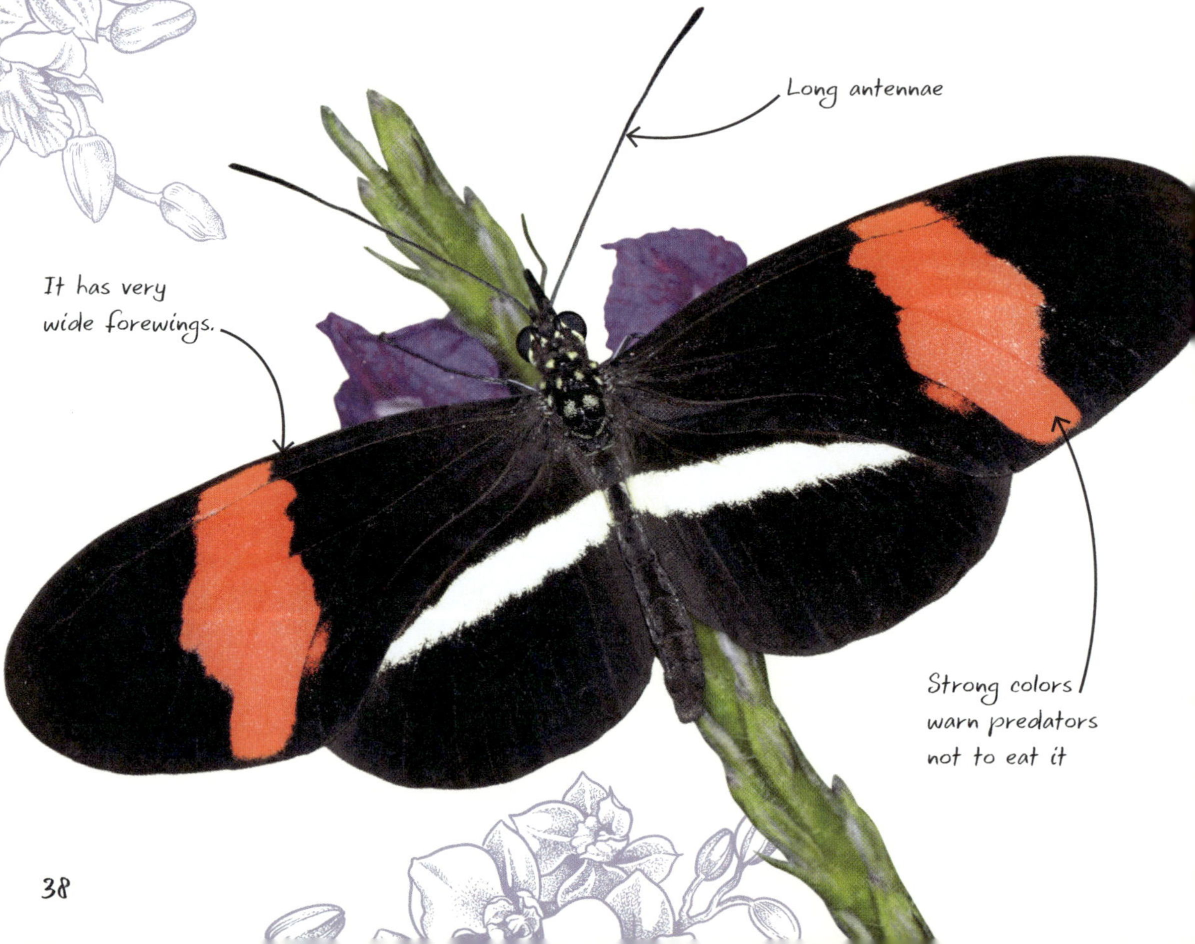
Long antennae
It has very wide forewings.
Strong colors warn predators not to eat it

Large wings and a slender body make the tree nymph a weak flier.

It has delicate, translucent wings.

Tree nymph

Idea leuconoe

This large, delicate butterfly looks like it is made of paper, so it is also sometimes called the "paper kite" or "rice paper" butterfly. The tree nymph flies slowly, with a gentle flapping, and is in no hurry to escape predators. This is because its obvious pale color serves as a warning to possible predators that it is packed with poisons and tastes horrible.

Notes

- Native to Southeast Asia
- Caterpillar collects and stores poisons from its food-plant, and these stay when it turns into an adult butterfly

Up to 4 in (100 mm)

Black-and-white,
spiked caterpillar

Zebra longwing

Heliconius charithonia

The striking black-and-white bars break up the outline of the zebra longwing butterfly when it is resting. This helps with camouflage, so it does not need to worry too much about predators. Another reason it does not need to worry is that, like other bright, tropical butterflies, the zebra longwing stores poisons. These are collected from the food-plant by the caterpillar, so birds avoid the caterpillar because of its bitter taste.

The black-and-white
markings across the
wings are similar to
that of a zebra.

Despite its
flimsy body, it
is a good flier.

Notes

- Lives in India, China, Japan, and Southeast Asia
- Males of this species are smaller than the females

Large, pale blotches look like eyes

Wings' edges with parallel ripple lines

Owl moth

Brahmaea wallichii

The bold pattern of this moth looks like it is edged with ripples, which help it to blend into any tree trunk that it likes to rest on during the day. If disturbed, the owl moth shakes itself backward and forward—this allows it to blur its shape and confuse a predator.

Up to 2 in (50 mm)

The moth's smooth outline is broken by its stark pattern.

There are usually 24–30 points radiating from the central blotch on the wing.

Radial moth

Apsarasa radians

This pretty moth is very strongly colored, yet when it is resting with its wings folded together over its back it is difficult to see. The radial moth looks spiny or prickly, and not at all mothlike! It can take on the appearance of a spiny caterpillar or even part of a spiked plant to keep from being eaten. Amazingly, the radial moth caterpillar is yet to be discovered!

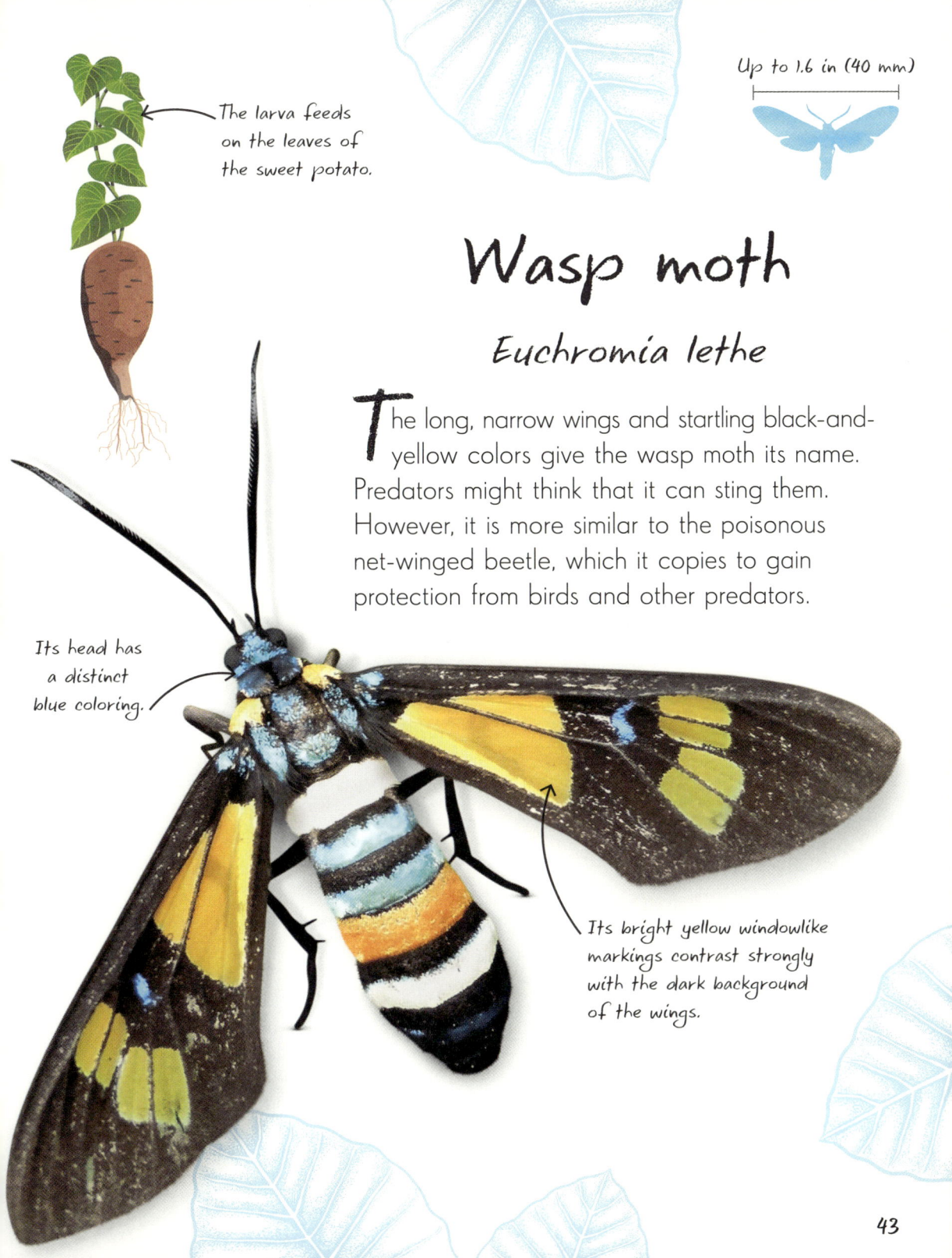

The larva feeds on the leaves of the sweet potato.

Up to 1.6 in (40 mm)

Wasp moth

Euchromia lethe

The long, narrow wings and startling black-and-yellow colors give the wasp moth its name. Predators might think that it can sting them. However, it is more similar to the poisonous net-winged beetle, which it copies to gain protection from birds and other predators.

Its head has a distinct blue coloring.

Its bright yellow windowlike markings contrast strongly with the dark background of the wings.

Up to 3 in (76 mm)

Red-bodied swallowtail

Pachliopta polydorus

The chrysalis looks like a twist of dead leaf, or it has been said to look like a cluster of flower buds.

Swallowtails get their name from the long tail on each hind wing. However, the red-bodied swallowtail has no tails—instead, it has a short bulge. The front wings are covered in dark, dusty scales that seem to change from black to gray when the light reflects at different angles. Sometimes these butterflies are called "greasies," because they look like they have been dipped in oil or grease!

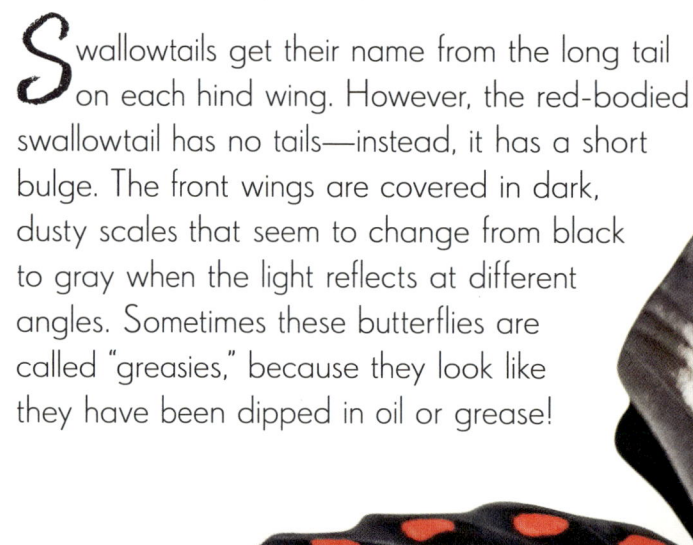

Long, narrow front wings

Rounded hind wings with a wavy outline

Common mormon

Papilio polytes

The male of the common mormon butterfly is always black, and it has a series of white spots across the wings. The females, however, have three different patterns. One form is black and white, like the male. Another pattern has cream streaks and red spots, and a third has white flashes and red spots.

Notes

• Lives in India and China through to Southeast Asia

• Thrives in agricultural areas because the caterpillars can eat leaves of cultivated orange or lime trees

This form of the female is white and red.

Up to 1.4 in (35 mm)

The front wings are long and angular at the corners.

Orange albatross

Appias nero

This is the only butterfly in the world that is completely orange. Males often gather together in large numbers to drink water and take in nutrients from mud at the side of streams—a behavior called puddling. Females prefer to stay high in the treetops.

There are only four walking legs. The front pair of legs are tiny, feathery fluffs used to help clean the antennae.

This butterfly has metallic-blue spots on its body and wings.

Notes

· Lives in Central and South America

· The cracking sound is also used to communicate with a potential mate

Queen cracker butterfly

Hamadryas arethusa

Males of this pretty checkered butterfly perch, head downward, on a tree trunk and guard it as their territory. If another male should pass by, it flies up, making a loud cracking sound—like a handclap—by striking together thickened veins on its front wings. The queen cracker butterfly also makes these sounds to startle a predator if any large, scary shape approaches, or even if butterflies of other species pass by.

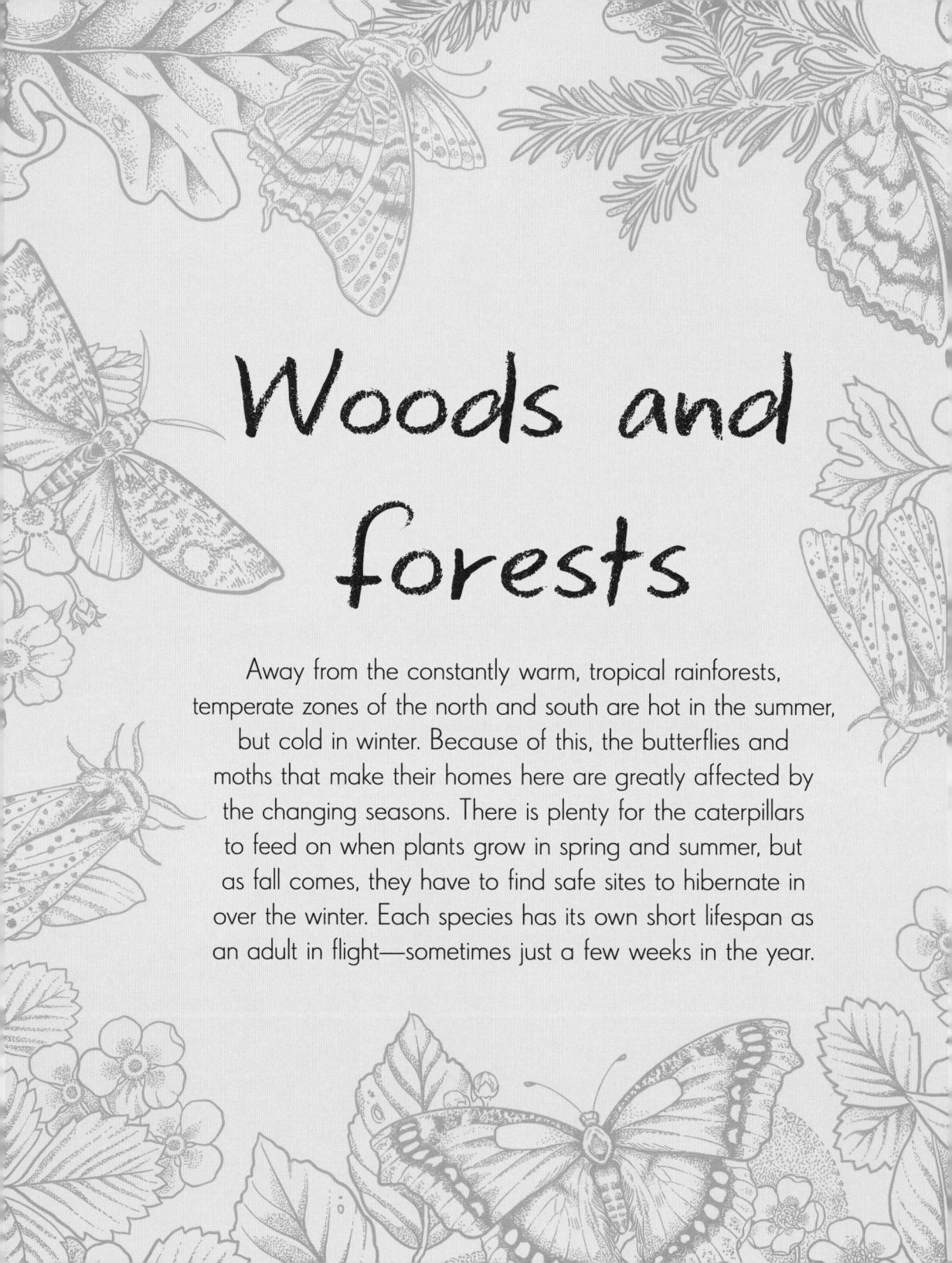

Woods and forests

Away from the constantly warm, tropical rainforests, temperate zones of the north and south are hot in the summer, but cold in winter. Because of this, the butterflies and moths that make their homes here are greatly affected by the changing seasons. There is plenty for the caterpillars to feed on when plants grow in spring and summer, but as fall comes, they have to find safe sites to hibernate in over the winter. Each species has its own short lifespan as an adult in flight—sometimes just a few weeks in the year.

Monarch

Danaus plexippus

Every year, monarch butterflies travel, or migrate, completely across North America to breed. The butterflies lay their eggs, then soon die, but the caterpillars quickly feed and hatch into new adults. In the fall, the new adults fly south to a tiny valley in Mexico. Here, over winter, they gather in their millions and hang from the branches of oyamel fir trees. There are so many butterflies bunched together that their combined weight can break the branches of the trees.

Monarchs rest high up on the branches of oyamel fir trees, clustering together with wings folded.

Large, broad wings make the monarch a strong flier.

Up to 1.4 in (35 mm)

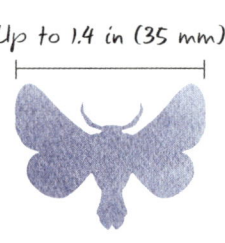

Oak processionary moth

Thaumetopoea processionea

This moth gets its wonderful name from the caterpillars, which live together in groups of around 20 to 100. They huddle together on an oak tree trunk during the day and crawl up into the branches to feed at night. As they move, the caterpillars leave strands of silk behind them, and in the morning, they will follow the silk lines back to their daytime cluster. When they are ready to become pupas, the caterpillars climb down the tree to nest lower down. They form a long line—a procession—with those behind following the silk threads laid down by the caterpillars at the front.

Notes

• Found throughout Europe, north Africa, and in parts of Asia

• Caterpillars are covered in thousands of long bristles, which are hollow and contain stinging venom

The mottled gray of the adult moth gives it camouflage when it rests on a tree trunk.

Up to 4.7 in (120 mm)

The pattern on the moth's wings matches the wrinkled, lichen-covered bark of old trees.

Goat moth

Cossus cossus

This large moth gets its interesting name from its caterpillars. The large, reddish-orange larvae burrow into the solid heartwood of old oak, willow, and poplar trees. The burrows, full of caterpillar droppings, sawdust, and oozing sap, become infected with yeasts and molds and smell very strongly like goats. Wood is low in nutrients, so it takes around 3–5 years for a caterpillar to become fully grown enough to turn into an adult.

Its caterpillar has a goatlike odor, which gives the moth its name.

Colors and patterns

Both butterflies and moths can have bright colors and beautiful patterns. Strong colors might seem like they would attract the attention of enemies, such as birds and other predators, but they are also a warning. Butterflies and moths also find color patterning useful when searching for a mate.

The cinnabar flies in the daytime. It is ignored by birds because its red-and-black colors warn them that they will feel sick if they try to eat one.

Warning!

As with brightly colored bees and wasps, strong colors warn of danger—not of a sting in the tail, but of a body full of poisons and horrible-tasting chemicals. So, birds and other animals soon learn to avoid these strongly patterned butterflies and moths.

White is just as strong a warning as black and red. As a caterpillar, the cabbage white feeds on strong-tasting cabbages, and from this it collects chemicals that help keep predators at bay.

Many butterflies and moths, such as the birdwing butterfly, have different color patterns between males and females.

Male and female birdwings can vary in size as well—the male is slightly smaller.

Female Cairns birdwing butterfly

Male Cairns birdwing butterfly

Finding a mate

Butterflies and moths have large eyes, and many can see well enough to distinguish colors and patterns in each other. Each species has its own special combination of color patterning, although these are sometimes difficult for humans to tell apart. This helps individuals of the same species find each other when they need to mate.

Insect's view

Unlike human eyes, insect eyes do not give a photographic image of the world, but they are good at recognizing movement, shapes, and patterns.

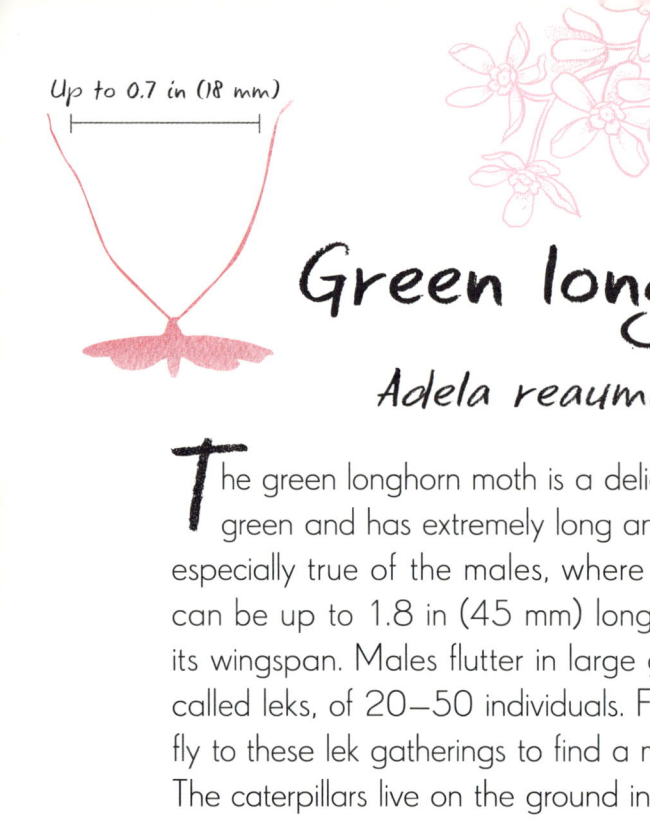

Up to 0.7 in (18 mm)

Green longhorn

Adela reaumurella

The green longhorn moth is a delicate, metallic green and has extremely long antennae. This is especially true of the males, where the antennae can be up to 1.8 in (45 mm) long—about twice its wingspan. Males flutter in large groups, called leks, of 20–50 individuals. Females fly to these lek gatherings to find a mate. The caterpillars live on the ground in leaf litter, feeding on dead leaves.

The antennae can appear white, glinting in the sunshine.

The color of their forewings is either bronze or metallic green.

The buff-tip of the wing is curved, like the edge of a broken twig.

Up to 2.7 in (68 mm)

Notes

• Feeds on the leaves of oak and other trees

• Bristly caterpillars eat together in a group

Buff-tip moth

Phalera bucephala

When the buff-tip moth rests with its wings curled over its body, it looks just like a bit of twig bark. The buff-tip of its name refers to the pale brown-and-cream blotch at its wingtip, which looks a lot like the broken wood found under the thin bark. The moth's flat, pale head has the appearance of the other end of the broken twig.

Up to 2.8 in (70 mm)

There are fewer white markings on the adults that fly in the spring.

Clear black-and-white fringes on the wings

Map

Araschnia levana

The map butterfly gets its name from the pattern of bright white lines on its underside, which look like roads marked on a map. Having lived through the winter months, caterpillars develop into bright orange-and-black adults in spring—a patterning called "form *levana*." These spring butterflies lay eggs, and the hatching caterpillars feed quickly to emerge as summer butterflies, with a completely different pattern—black, but with a strong bar of white across the wings. This pattern is called "form *prorsa*."

Notes

· Caterpillars feed on stinging nettles

· They live across Europe and Asia

· They have two different color and pattern forms, called dimorphism

Lobster moth
Stauropus fagi

The lobster moth is named after its peculiar caterpillar, with its large, swollen tail and strangely angled front legs, which look like pincers. Writers in ancient times described it as being half-spider and half-scorpion! Although it looks odd, it is completely harmless. The caterpillar does not have the normal tube shape, which may help it to escape predators, such as birds, that hunt for things they recognize as edible.

The mottled brown moth is well camouflaged against tree bark.

The lobster moth caterpillar does not look like a caterpillar— it looks more like a twisted bit of dead leaf or twig!

The fat tail has two long horns that look like stingers, but they have no venom and are harmless.

The front legs are clawlike.

57

Orange-tip

Anthocharis cardamines

The orange-tip butterfly is aptly named, yet only the males actually possess the bright-orange wing tips. They may use them for display to mark their territory and to attract a mate. The females have mottled-black wing corners, which help with camouflage when they rest on flowers in the dappled light along woodland edges. The chrysalis is a striking, pointed, thornlike structure that looks like a plant shoot.

Only the male has the bright orange wing-tip mark.

Notes

· Found throughout Europe and northern Asia

· Springtime butterfly of woodland edges, hedgerows, and forest clearings

The adult moth is brown and well-hidden when resting on a tree trunk.

Up to 1.7 in (43 mm)

The bright colors warn predators not to try and eat it.

Saddleback moth

Acharia stimulea

The saddleback moth gets its name from the brightly colored caterpillar, which is purplish-brown, but has a large, bright-green saddlelike mark across its back. The caterpillar has fleshy horns at each end, and these are covered in sharp, stinging spines that can cause a painful, swollen rash on human skin.

Up to 4 in (100 mm)

Mourning cloak
Nymphalis antiopa

This beautiful butterfly gets its name from its deep color—like a cloak worn to a funeral, but with pale clothes showing underneath. The butterfly is also called Camberwell beauty. This is because it is a rare migrant to the British Isles, and the first time it was discovered there was in 1748 in the small village of Camberwell, now part of southeast London.

Notes

• Adult butterflies can live for 11–12 months, one of the longest butterfly lifespans known

• These powerful fliers will fly hundreds of miles out of their normal breeding areas

The pale edge can range from bright white to cream.

The blue marks vary from round blotches to tiny spots, or may even be absent entirely.

With its fluffy front legs and body, the moth looks like a furry growth on bark.

Puss moth

Cerura vinula

When resting on a tree trunk, with wings furled together, the hairy body of the puss moth makes it look a bit catlike. The black-and-white zigzags help it blend into the mottled tree bark. If the large, fat caterpillar is disturbed, it hunches up, presents a threatening red head, and extends two long, thin, spiny tails. These tails are harmless, but as a last resort, the caterpillar can squirt stinging formic acid from glands in its neck.

The dark saddle mark helps break up the outline of the caterpillar, making it harder for predators to spot.

It has bright-to-pale-green forewings.

Green oak tortrix moth

Tortrix viridana

The green oak tortrix moth is very common, but because it is small and its caterpillars feed high up in oak trees, it is easily overlooked. Sometimes there are huge population explosions, and millions of caterpillars strip whole woodlands of their leaves, damaging the oak trees. At these times, caterpillar droppings—called frass—fall and hit the dead leaves on the woodland floor. There are so many droppings that they sound like gentle rain as they fall.

If disturbed, the caterpillar drops off the leaf, but hangs, swinging by a silk thread, to avoid the danger.

Bird-cherry ermine

Yponomeuta evonymella

The bird-cherry ermine moth is spotted like the ermine fur once used to edge the luxurious cloaks of kings and queens. The caterpillars live together in large clusters on the plants they feed from, and they create a protective web of silk in which to hide. Sometimes whole trees, or even hedgerows, can be covered in the white webs, and all the leaves of the trees are eaten away.

Notes

• Caterpillars feed on the bird cherry, a tree often planted for its flowers rather than its fruit

• Closely related species of moths also attack cultivated cherries and apples and can be major farmland pests

The moth curls its wings around its body when at rest.

Up to 3.5 in (90 mm)

Purple emperor

Apatura iris

This elegant purple butterfly flies high around the tops of large oak trees. It has a short, stout tongue, and, although it does not drink nectar from flowers, the butterfly can be tempted down by butterfly-spotters with a range of smelly baits. Lots of different baits work—from rotten shrimp and old banana skins to moldy cheese and animal droppings.

The male butterfly has a deep purple sheen.

Notes

• Found in Europe and northern Asia

• Caterpillar feeds on leaves of sallow trees

• Female is black and white in color

It also feeds on the minerals and salts found in moist ground.

The furry caterpillars feed on the leaves of trees such as hawthorn.

Up to 3.5 in (90 mm)

Lappet

Gastropacha quercifolia

When it rests, the lappet holds its front and back wings at different angles, and it looks just like a curled, dead leaf. Even the markings on its wings look like the veins of a leaf, and its wing edges are wrinkled to complete the illusion.

The moth's resemblance to a leaf helps it to hide from predators.

This moth has a protruding snout.

Up to 0.3 in (8 mm)

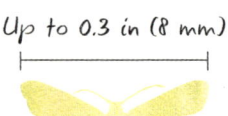

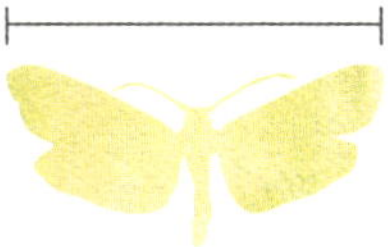

Scribbly gum moth

Ogmograptis scribula

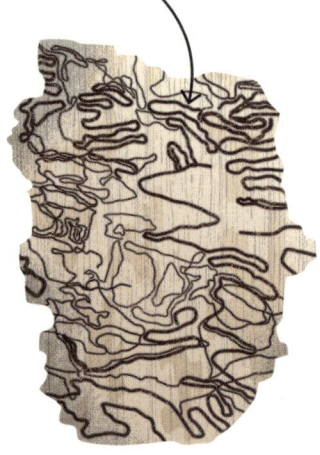

This small, silvery moth lays its eggs on the bark of eucalyptus gum trees. As it feeds, the caterpillar chews narrow burrows under the bark. Many years later, when the tree bark peels away and falls off, the winding tunnels are revealed and look like pen scribbles on the wood.

The dark lines show where caterpillars chewed through the bark.

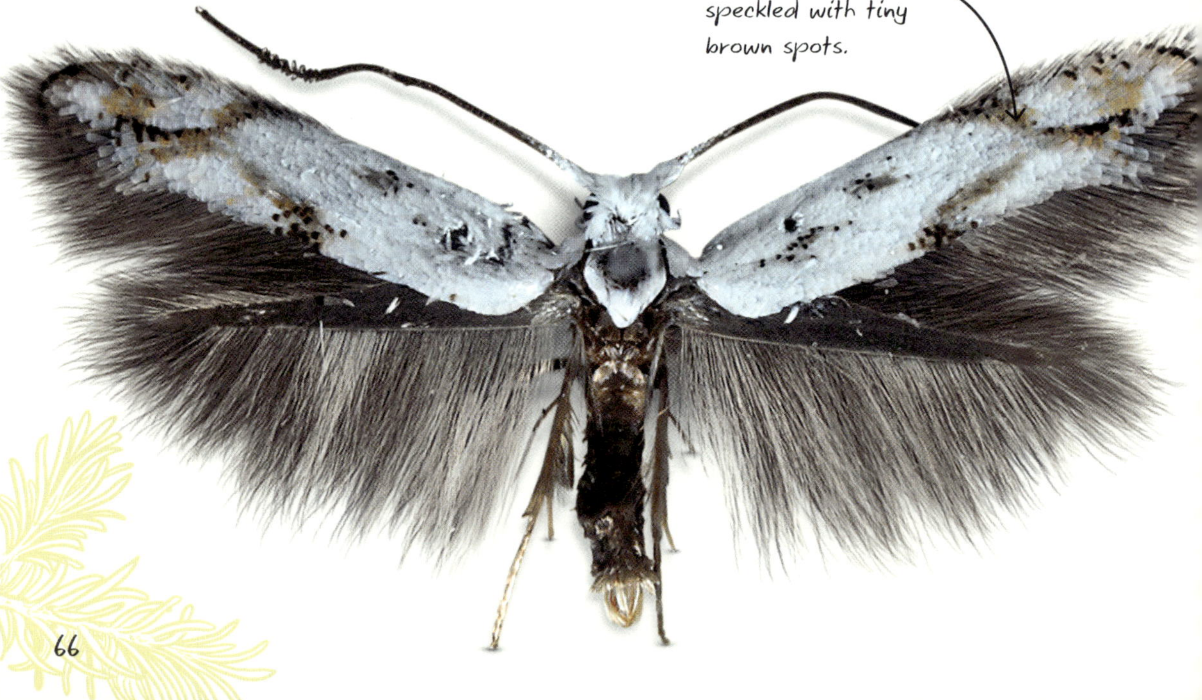

The silvery moth is speckled with tiny brown spots.

A fast, strong flier, this moth uses its long, narrow wings to fly for hundreds of miles.

Up to 4.3 in (110 mm)

The irregular blotches and streaks of color help break up the moth's outline, making it hard for predators to spot.

Oleander hawk moth

Daphnis nerii

This beautiful hawk moth is patterned with delicate swirls of purplish pink, green, and grayish brown. If settled on a fence or wall, it looks brightly patterned and very striking, but when it rests on leaves with its wings angled backward, the colors give it perfect camouflage and it is very difficult to see.

Up to 2 in (50 mm)

The short, black bars look like legs and antennae at the "wrong" end of the moth.

Picasso moth

Baorisa hieroglyphica

When the Picasso moth rests with its wings together, the short, black bars at the wing tips look like legs, and the red-tinged oval blotches look like eyes. This gives the impression that its head is actually where its tail is. This is useful, as it can confuse a predator, making it unsure which end to sneak up on to launch its attack.

Notes

· Lives in northern India and Southeast Asia

· The moth gets its name from the Spanish artist Pablo Picasso, who used striking designs and bright colors in his paintings

Bramble leaf-miner

Stigmella aurella

This little moth is easy to overlook. Its caterpillars are so tiny that they burrow through the middle of a leaf, leaving a pale tunnel behind where they have eaten the greenery. The caterpillar is like a miner boring through the plant, and, in fact, this type of feeding is called leaf mining.

Mine left by the caterpillar in a bramble leaf.

The tiny moth has a white bar across its wings.

Up to 4 in (100 mm)

Two-tailed pasha

Charaxes jasius

This beautiful butterfly is a strong and fast flier. Males and females gather at prominent rocky hilltops, where they fly around each other to find mates. The butterflies are attracted to rotting fruits. There are two generations each year—the late summer butterflies are larger than those that arrive in the early spring.

Notes

- Lives in southern Mediterranean regions of Europe and in Africa
- The caterpillars eat the leaves of the strawberry tree

There are two tails on each back wing.

The complicated pattern helps break up the outline of the butterfly when it is roosting.

Adult moth sitting
on a sleeping bird

Up to 2 in (52 mm)

When extended, the sharp,
tubelike tongue is tipped
with hooks, which grip the
edges of the bird's eyelids.

Teardrop moth

Hemiceratoides hieroglyphica

The teardrop moth is known for visiting sleeping
birds at night and drinking the teardrops from
their eyes. In addition to the water, the moth gets
nutrients in the form of salts and also proteins from
the fluid. Elsewhere in the world, there are other types
of moth that drink the tears of crocodiles or deer.

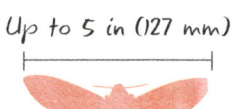

Up to 5 in (127 mm)

Death's-head hawk moth

Acherontia atropos

At rest, with wings held together, the mottled pattern of its body and wings allows the death's-head hawk moth to hide from predators. Although the skull-like pattern is there to help with camouflage, it has led people to create myths about the moth being bad luck or a sinister sign of death. The death's-head hawk moth has a short, tough, hollow tongue that it uses to suck honey from beehives, and it can also blow air down it to make a whistling sound—which just adds to the superstitious stories that have grown up around it.

Its skull-like shape gives the moth its name.

If disturbed, the moth flicks open its front wings, displaying the bright-yellow back wings to startle any attacker.

Fields and grasslands

Open habitats such as fields, meadows, and savannas can be a draw for butterflies and moths. These areas are often more flowery than shaded woodlands and forests, and the wide spaces are sunny and bright. However, there are fewer places for butterflies and moths to hide, unless the insects settle in the grass. Grassland and savanna habitats include some types of farmland, as well as places where wild animals graze.

Up to 1.5 in (38 mm)

Long legs allow the
moth to hang in
the long grass.

White
plume moth

Pterophorus pentadactyla

As its name suggests, this small, pretty moth is
pure white. By day, it always rests with its
narrow, featherlike wings held out away from
its body. It hardly looks like a moth, and more
closely resembles a piece of broken dead grass or
perhaps a feather—a clever piece of camouflage
deception. The white plume moth flies at night,
visiting flowers to take nectar.

Painted lady

Vanessa cardui

The painted lady is perhaps the most widespread butterfly in the world. This is because it flies great distances each year from its overwintering sites in North America, north Africa, and central Asia to spread out across Europe, Asia, Central America, and parts of Australia. Yearly migrations follow warm, seasonal winds, and the painted lady's arrival in new territories is marked by the sudden influx of butterflies flying around flowers.

The checkered underside has a flash of bright pinkish-orange.

Notes

• Yearly migrations are sometimes so dramatic that they make national news headlines

• Caterpillars feed on thistle leaves

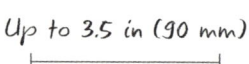

Swallowtail

Papilio machaon

The swallowtail gets its name from the tails at the tips of its back wings. There are more than 40 different forms and varieties of this butterfly. Slight differences in the shapes and darkness of the blue-and-black markings have been described. This butterfly occurs all across the northern hemisphere and spans four continents—North America, Europe, north Africa, and northern Asia.

Notes

· The brightly colored caterpillar warns birds and other predators that it contains foul-tasting chemicals it has collected from its food-plants

· Also known as the Old World swallowtail in the United States

The large wings make this butterfly a strong flier able to migrate many hundreds of miles.

Up to 1.6 in (40 mm)

Black spots form a
distinctive pattern
on the upper wings

Large blue

Phengaris arion

When the tiny caterpillars of the large blue butterfly hatch from their eggs, they start feeding on the leaves of thyme plants. They then produce a chemical scent that attracts red ants. The ants take the caterpillars back to their underground nest. The caterpillars then start to eat the ant grubs. Afterward, each caterpillar produces a special liquid from glands in its back that the ants drink.

The ants ignore the caterpillars in their nest.

Clever disguises

Like all small creatures, butterflies and moths are always in danger of being eaten by something larger. Hiding from enemies by blending into the natural patterns and colors of grass, leaves, tree bark, or lichen-covered rocks is a good way of avoiding these dangers.

How caterpillars hide

Many caterpillars are streaked with pale lines on a green or brown background. This helps them blend in when they rest against a grass stem, plant stalk, or the midrib of a leaf. Other caterpillars look like bird droppings or bits of dead leaf, so they do not appear very tempting to other animals.

Caterpillars usually feed at night and stay still against a suitable background during the day, when their enemies are hunting.

By holding on only with its back prolegs, the caterpillar of the geometer moth looks just like a twig.

Blending in

Mottled or broken patterns help a moth or butterfly disappear into the background. The irregular pattern of blotches and speckles looks just like the crusty surface on which the insect rests. These patterns also break up the outline silhouette of the insect—predatory birds hunt by looking for insect-shaped food items, and their eyes are confused by the wavy patterns and broken color patches.

If resting during the day, remaining camouflaged against a speckled background is an important tactic when predators are hunting for you.

The grayling butterfly is known for resting on bare sandy or rocky ground that exactly matches its patterning.

Up to 2.4 in (60 mm)

Distinctive orange bands on the forewings

The size and color of the eyespots vary.

Buckeye

Junonia coenia

The large eyespots make this butterfly easy to recognize when it settles on the ground to bask in the sunshine. It is thought that the buckeye gets some protection from inexperienced predators, such as young birds. This is because the birds see the false eyes and imagine the butterfly to be a much larger animal, too big for them to attack!

Notes

· Found in North America

· Caterpillars are black and spiny and feed on many different types of plant

Up to 2.2 in (56 mm)

Grayling

Hipparchia semele

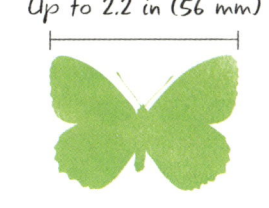

The grayling butterfly lives in dry, sandy and rocky places without much vegetation. When the butterfly rests on the ground, it closes its wings and the camouflaged undersides help it hide. For a further trick, the butterfly tilts its folded wings toward the sun so that it casts only the smallest shadow, and this makes the insect even harder for predators to spot.

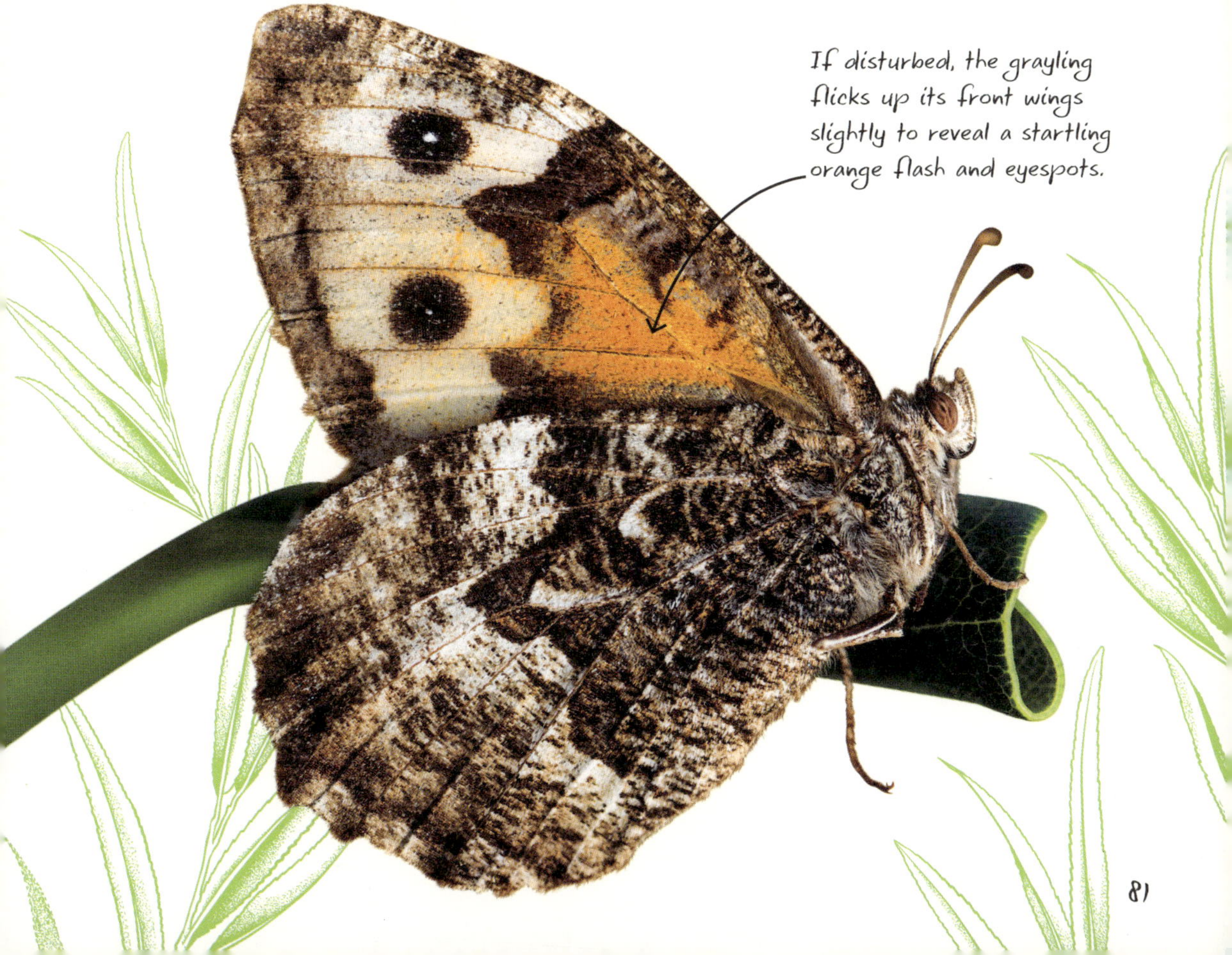
If disturbed, the grayling flicks up its front wings slightly to reveal a startling orange flash and eyespots.

Up to 1.6 in (40 mm)

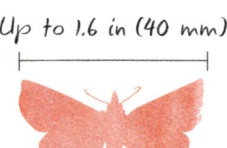

Vampire moth

Calyptra eustrigata

The aptly named vampire moth has a short, sharp, and stout tongue. Similar moth species use the tongue to pierce fruit to suck out the juices. However, the vampire moth also sometimes pierces the skin of water buffalo, tapir, and deer to suck their blood. At first, many people found this strange behavior hard to believe, until it was tested—caged moths were offered a human finger to bite…

This moth's barbed tongue helps it pierce the skin of mammals.

Its forewings have pointed tips.

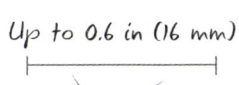

There are actually 24 plumes
(six on each of the four
wings), but when the moth
rests, these are sometimes
difficult to count.

Twenty-plumed moth

Alucita hexadactyla

Butterfly and moth wings have tubular veins that give strength to wing membranes when the insects fly. But in the twenty-plumed moth, the veins are separated—each into a long, thin plume. The veins are fringed with hairs, making each wing look like it has several feathers rather than one.

83

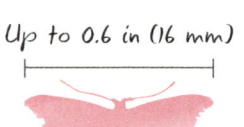

Case-bearing moth

Coleophora albidella

This small, slim, silvery moth is secretive as an adult and is easy to miss. The caterpillar, however, has a big appetite and feeds on sallow leaves. It makes a sock-shaped case out of bits of dead leaves and its own droppings, held together with strands of black silk. Only the caterpillar's front legs and mouthparts stick out, so as it walks about, grazing on the leaves, it looks like a piece of dead plant or a bird dropping. This protects it from predators.

The caterpillar even covers the outside of the case with hairs and bristles from the leaves' surface.

The adult moth is mostly white, but can sometimes have darker, hazy speckling.

Black spot in center of the forewing

Hind wings of the male are brighter than the female's

California dogface

Zerene eurydice

The California dogface is a brightly colored butterfly that gets its name from the yellow-and-black markings on its forewings, which look like a dog's pointed snout, complete with open mouth and eyespot. Only the male has this pattern—the female butterfly is entirely yellow, except for the black spot of the dog's eye.

Notes

- Found in California

- Very strong and fast flier

- Caterpillars feed on the leaves of false indigo plants

Up to 2 in (55 mm)

Bogong moth
Agrotis infusa

Hind-wing fringes are glossy and pale.

Every year in Australia, the adult bogong moths migrate to the cool mountains—including Mount Bogong—to spend the hot, dry summer period sheltering together in large numbers in caves and rock hollows. Traditionally, the moths were collected by the Aboriginal people of Australia. The moths were roasted, then ground into a paste to make "moth-meat" cakes, which have a nutty taste and are full of protein.

Gathering together in the cool, humid caves, the moths protect themselves from drying out and dying.

Nine-spotted moth

Amata phegea

There is no mistaking this strangely patterned moth, which is inky blue-black, with usually nine bright-white spots on its wings and two yellow bands across its body. The moth flies during the day and its bright colors warn predators not to eat it because it tastes horrible!

There are six spots on each front wing and three on each back wing, making a total of nine on each side.

Notes

• Lives in Europe and central Asia

• White-spot burnet looks very similar to this moth, even though it is not closely related

Up to 1.7 in (45 mm)

Cinnabar

Tyria jacobaeae

This bright, red-and-black moth flies actively during the day. Its equally brightly colored caterpillars feed on ragwort. Sometimes, there are so many caterpillars that they strip the plant of all its leaves, and there is nothing left for them to eat. If this happens, they never grow large enough to transform into adults and the population in the area crashes.

Notes

· Found in Europe and Asia

· Deliberately released into North America, Australia, and New Zealand to try and control ragwort, which has become a notorious, invasive weed in these areas

· Caterpillars store poisons collected from the plants they eat

The moth is named for its red color, which is similar to the red rock known as cinnabar.

Bull's-eye moth

Automeris io

Up to 3.3 in (85 mm)

When this large moth rests on a tree trunk, it looks exactly like the mottled-brown color of the wrinkled bark or a dead leaf. However, if it is disturbed by a predator, it flicks open its front wings to reveal two bright eyespots that will make the enemy think it's facing a much bigger animal, and will be frightened away.

Feathered antennae

The eyespots may cause just a moment of hesitation in a predator, but this may be enough for the moth to take flight.

Up to 1.3 in (32 mm)

Bright colors are usually a warning for predators not to eat it.

Beetle moth
Lycomorpha pholus

W hen it settles, this moth looks like a net-winged beetle in size and shape. These brightly colored, black-and-red beetles occur in the same places as the beetle moths. The beetles contain high levels of poisons, which make them bad-tasting to predators. Because of this, predators stay away from both the beetles and the moths—even though the moths themselves are not actually poisonous.

The ends of the net-winged beetle's wing cases are black, just like the beetle moth.

While the mouthparts, or palps, are used by most insects for moving food around, how this moth uses them is unknown.

Hedge beauty

Alabonia geoffrella

Although tiny, this distinctive moth is beautifully and brightly colored when looked at under a lens. In addition to the pattern of black, orange, and white, the hedge beauty has streaks of pale metallic-blue scales along its wings. It flies during the day, fluttering round trees and bushes in preference to visiting flowers.

Notes

· Found in Europe

· Caterpillar feeds inside the stems of old bramble bushes or under the bark of dead tree trunks

Up to 2 in (50 mm)

Angle shades

Phlogophora meticulosa

When it rests, the wings of this unmistakeable brown, gold, pink, and green moth are held together, folded and wrinkled, forming a sharply cutout angle. The strong triangular marks on the moth's wings break up its outline, making it appear to vanish when it settles in dead grass, stems, or curled leaves.

Its colors and patterns make it look like a withered fall leaf.

A tuft of long scales behind the head creates a bulge that also helps disrupt the insect's outline in side view.

The male has a streak of special scent-carrying scales.

Up to 1.3 in (34 mm)

Large skipper

Ochlodes sylvanus

When they settle to rest, skippers do not hold their wings together like other butterflies. Instead, the insects hold their front wings upright, while the back wings are laid flat. This sometimes confuses people into thinking they are moths. The male has a long patch of dark scales on its front wings, which helps special scents secreted from glands underneath to waft into the air to attract a female.

Notes

· The scent-carrying scales on a butterfly's wings are called androconia

· Skippers are usually small butterflies, but the large skipper is so-called because it is the largest of this group in northern Europe

Up to 3 in (80 mm)

Emperor moth

Saturnia pavonia

The emperor moth occurs on heaths and moors, where its caterpillars feed on heather. When it spins its silk cocoon to protect the chrysalis, the caterpillar also creates a ring of outward-facing bristles at the head end. When the adult moth emerges, it can push past these bristles, but predators struggle to get in through the tight neck of spines.

The caterpillar is covered with bristly, yellow or orange warts.

Male wingspan up to 2.4 in (60 mm)

Up to 3.7 in (95 mm)

Apollo

Parnassius apollo

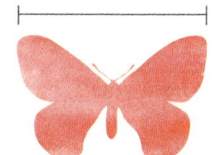

Apollo butterflies live high up on mountain meadows. Because mountains are separated by broad lowlands, which the butterflies do not cross, each mountain peak or range has its own specialized subspecies, with slightly different color patterns.

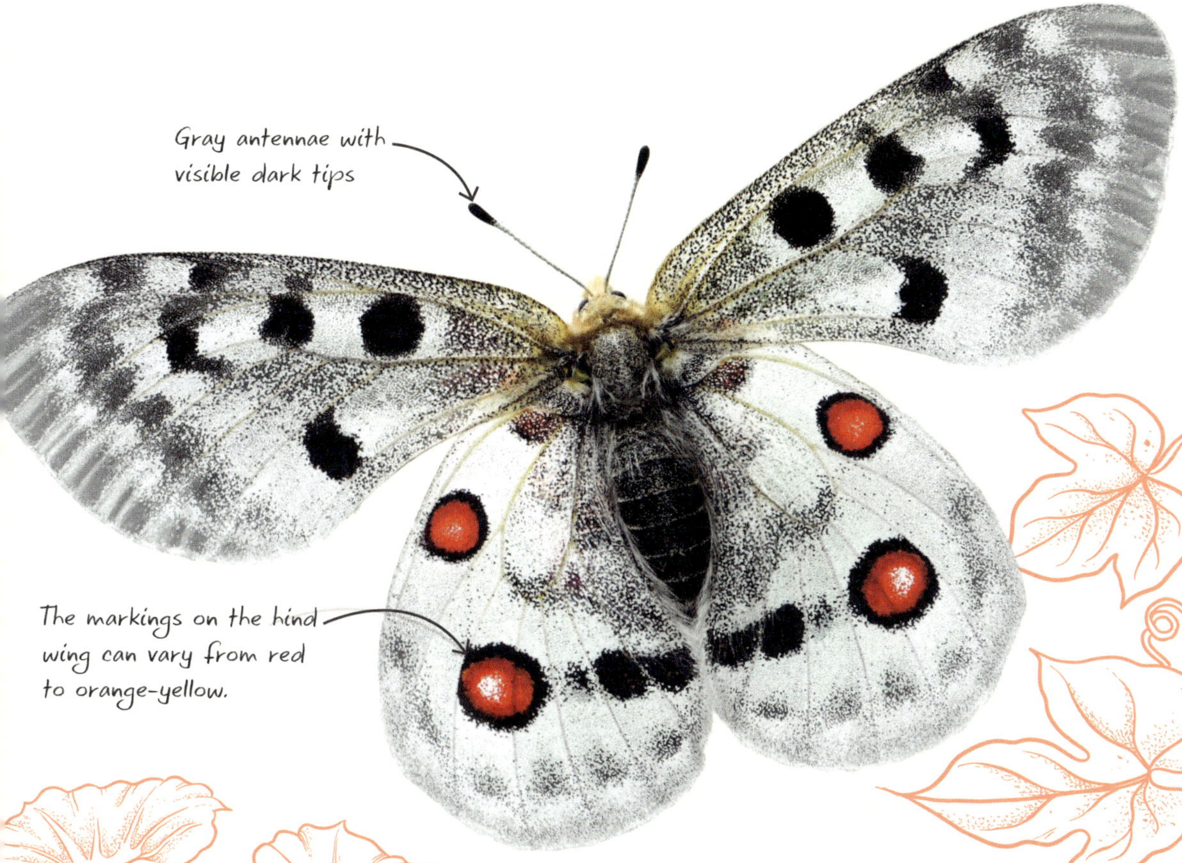
Gray antennae with visible dark tips
The markings on the hind wing can vary from red to orange-yellow.

Up to 1.2 in (30 mm)

The moth has a hairy body.

Notes

· Lives in southern and central Europe

· The mandolin moth's sound can be heard by the human ear

Mandolin moth

Rileyiana fovea

This ordinary-looking moth was one of the first to reveal that moths can produce sound to communicate. On the underside of its back wing, on a vein, the male mandolin moth has a small swelling and tiny raised pegs. When it rubs its back leg against these pegs, the rasping sound is made louder, or amplified, by the hollow swelling. This creates a buzzing "song," which is used as a mating call to the female of the species.

Pug moths rest with their wings spread out wide.

Up to 1.2 in (30 mm)

Hawaiian pug moth

Eupithecia orichloris

The caterpillar of this small pug moth is unique. Instead of feeding on leaves, it snatches at live flies with deadly accuracy and then eats them. The caterpillar clings to a leaf using its back legs and holds its long, narrow body upright. If a fly lands nearby, the caterpillar bends suddenly and uses its front legs to capture its prey.

The caterpillar uses its front legs to hold struggling prey, such as a fly.

Up to 1.3 in (32 mm)

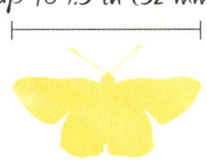

Duke of Burgundy

Hamearis lucina

The rather regally named Duke of Burgundy belongs to a group of butterflies called metalmarks. This is because there are small patches of bright, metallic scales found in many species within this group. The front legs of the males are very short and only used for cleaning the antennae. When the male butterflies perch, they appear to have only four walking legs.

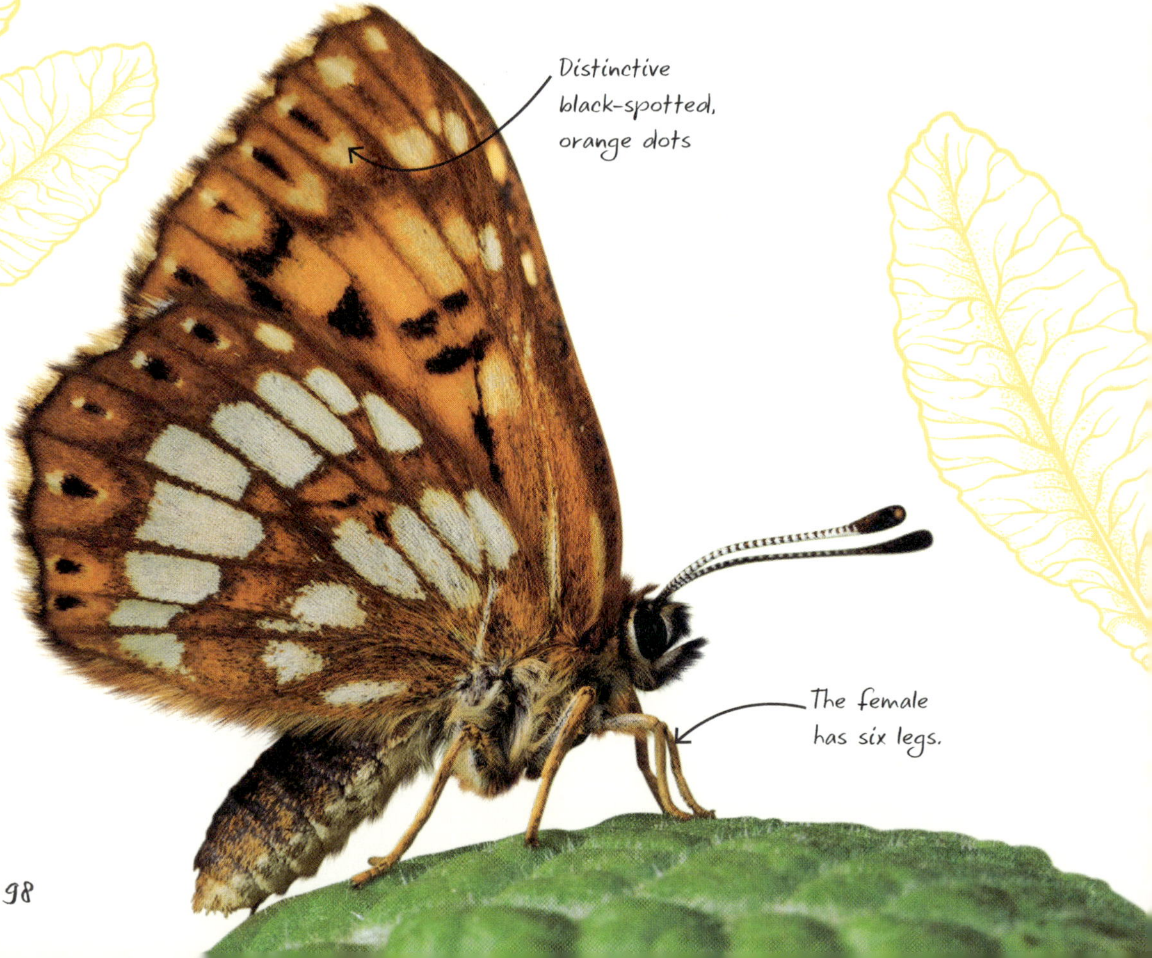
Distinctive black-spotted, orange dots
The female has six legs.

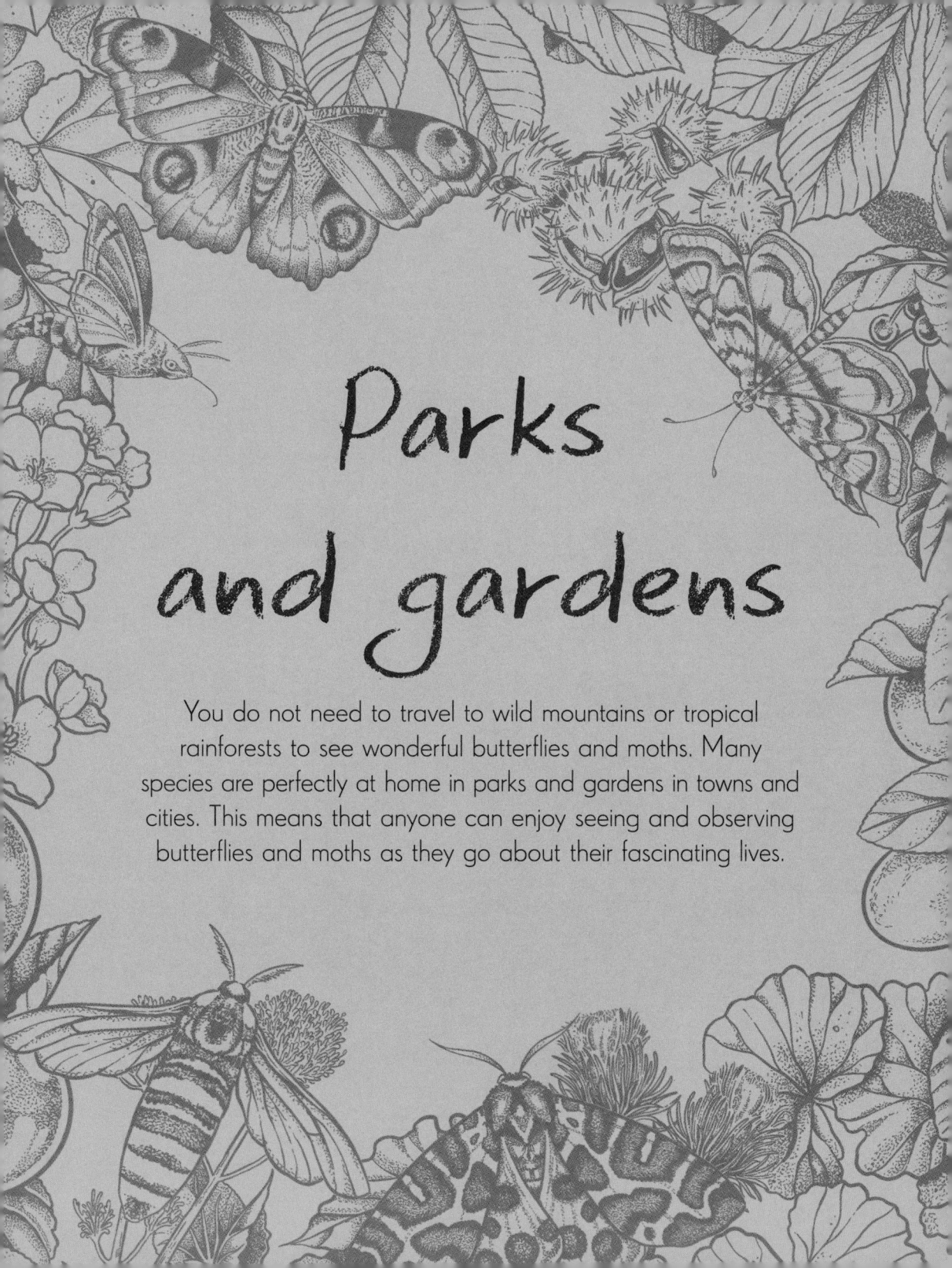

Parks
and gardens

You do not need to travel to wild mountains or tropical rainforests to see wonderful butterflies and moths. Many species are perfectly at home in parks and gardens in towns and cities. This means that anyone can enjoy seeing and observing butterflies and moths as they go about their fascinating lives.

Up to 2.5 in (63 mm)

Only the female has dark dots on the front wings, males just have dark corners.

Large cabbage white

Pieris brassicae

Cabbages contain strong-smelling chemicals, so people prefer to eat them after the leaves have been cooked. However, the caterpillars of cabbage-white butterflies store these chemicals so that the caterpillars will taste horrid to birds and other predators. Even when the caterpillars have developed into butterflies, the bright white of the adults tells the predators that they still taste bad.

The caterpillars feed together openly, without fear of being eaten, because they store poisons from the food-plant.

Up to 2 in (50 mm)

Hummingbird hawk moth

Macroglossum stellatarum

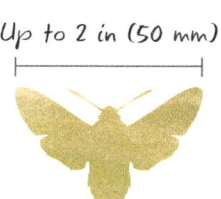

The wings of the hummingbird hawk moth beat so fast that they become a hazy blur to the human eye. And, like a hummingbird, the moth hovers in midair and uses its long, curved tongue to dip into flowers to drink nectar without the need to settle on the petals. This hawk moth is a strong flier and migrates north every year to dwell in new areas.

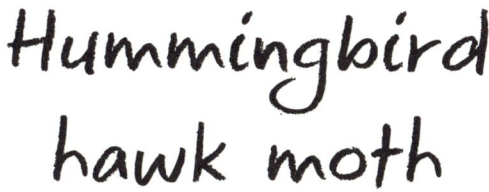

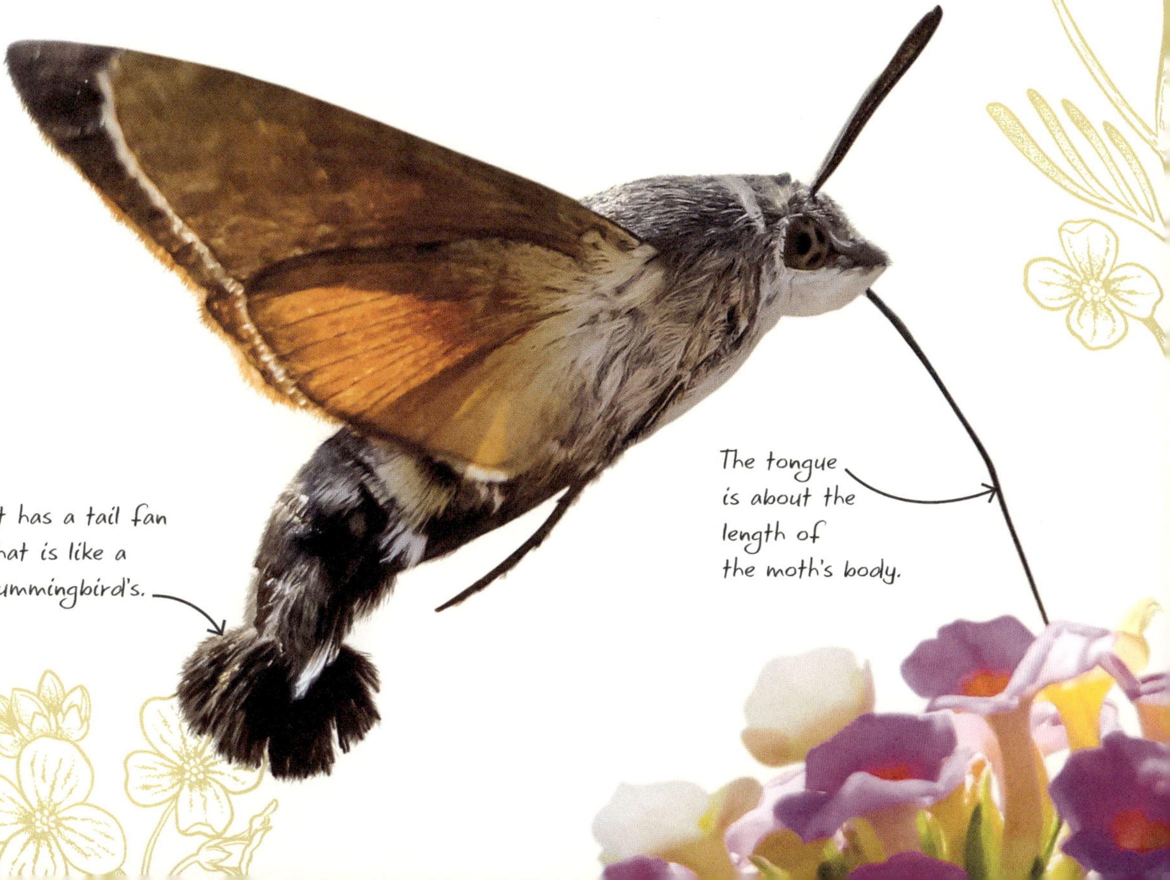
It has a tail fan that is like a hummingbird's.
The tongue is about the length of the moth's body.

Up to 0.4 in (9 mm)

Horse chestnut leaf-miner

Cameraria ohridella

The caterpillar of this pretty moth is so small that it feeds between the upper and lower layer of the horse-chestnut leaf, leaving a pale, air-filled blotch, or mine, as it goes. Each leaf can have up to 100 caterpillar mine-blotches on it. In fact, there can be so many mines in a leaf that the whole tree looks brown rather than green.

Horse chestnut trees can be badly damaged by caterpillars eating their leaves—but the trees will survive!

This tiny moth is rich brown in color and has bright white stripes.

The female with
its batch of eggs

Vaporer

Orgyia antiqua

The male has wings
like any normal moth
and flies at night and
in the daytime.

The female vaporer moth has no wings! When she emerges from her cocoon, a male flies in to mate, and then she lays about 300 doughnut-shaped eggs around the remains of her cocoon. The eggs then hatch into caterpillars, which are covered with bright tufts of long bristles and eat a wide variety of plants.

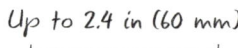

Elephant hawk moth

Deilephila elpenor

The elephant hawk moth gets its name from a trick its caterpillar pulls to make itself look dangerous. First, the caterpillar shrinks its front segments into what looks like a narrow elephant trunk. Next, it swells the segments just behind to enlarge the dark eyespot-markings to look like a head. This way it actually gets protection from predators by looking like a snake, rather than an elephant.

The swollen eyespots make the small caterpillar seem larger and more threatening than it is.

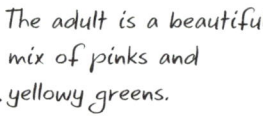

The adult is a beautiful mix of pinks and yellowy greens.

Hornet moth
Sesia apiformis

The hornet moth belongs to a group called clearwing moths. It has clear wings, with just a band of colored scales around the edges. Its body is banded with a black-and-yellow pattern, making it look like a wasp or hornet. This mimicry helps the moth frighten off potential predators. And the moth even moves with jerky, wasplike movements to add to the deception.

Its clear wings have dark veins.

Notes

· Lives mainly in Europe and parts of Asia and has been accidentally introduced into North America

· Maggotlike caterpillars burrow through the thick bark of old poplar trees

· Caterpillars take 2-4 years to grow large enough to change into adult moths

Up to 3 in (75 mm)

The back wings are usually orange with dark-blue spots, although some moths may have yellow colors.

Garden tiger

Arctia caja

The strong, bright colors of the adult tiger-moth's wings warn predators that it contains foul-tasting chemicals. If disturbed, the moth suddenly flicks open its bright hind wings to signal danger. The moth produces droplets of clear, yellow liquid filled with the chemicals contained in two glands behind its head.

Notes

• Found in North America and Europe

• Pattern of blotches and spots can vary so that no two specimens are exactly alike

Up to 0.9 in (22 mm)

The moth gets its name from its pattern, which looks like the factory mark on the underside of a fine China plate.

Beautiful china mark

Nymphula nitidulata

The small, pale caterpillars of this lovely moth feed on bur reed, a plant found growing at the edges of lakes and rivers. First, the caterpillar burrows into the stem of a plant. It then makes a tiny case out of the leaf and lives on the outside of the plant. Sometimes, the caterpillar feeds completely underwater.

The caterpillar's case is made from bits of cutout leaf spun together with silk. It contains an air bubble so the caterpillar can breathe underwater.

Up to 0.8 in (20 mm)

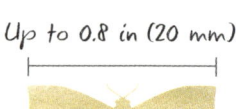

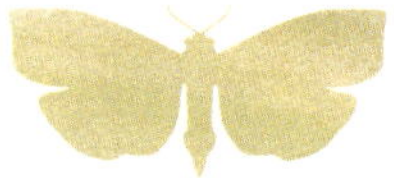

Codling moth

Cydia pomonella

The small codling moth lays its eggs on the fruit buds of apple and pear trees. The caterpillar burrows through the developing fruit. It mostly eats the seeds and core. When the apple falls from the tree, the caterpillar chews its way out to make a cocoon in the soil nearby.

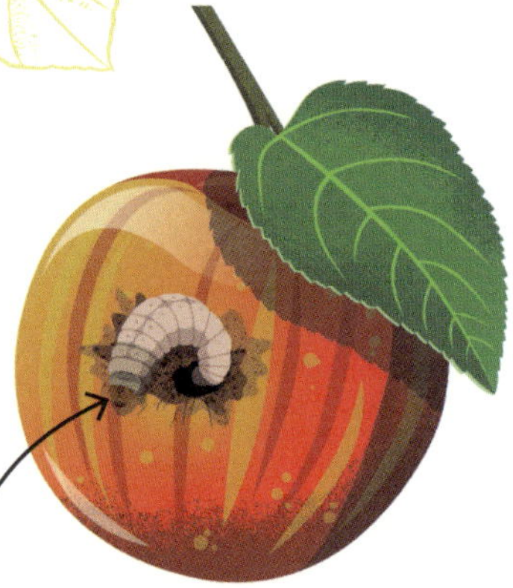

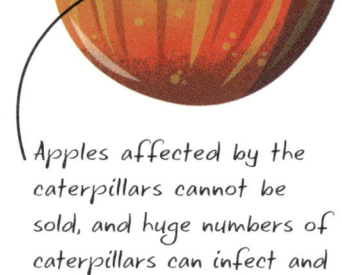

Apples affected by the caterpillars cannot be sold, and huge numbers of caterpillars can infect and destroy an apple crop.

The moth is perfectly camouflaged when it is resting on the trunk of the apple tree.

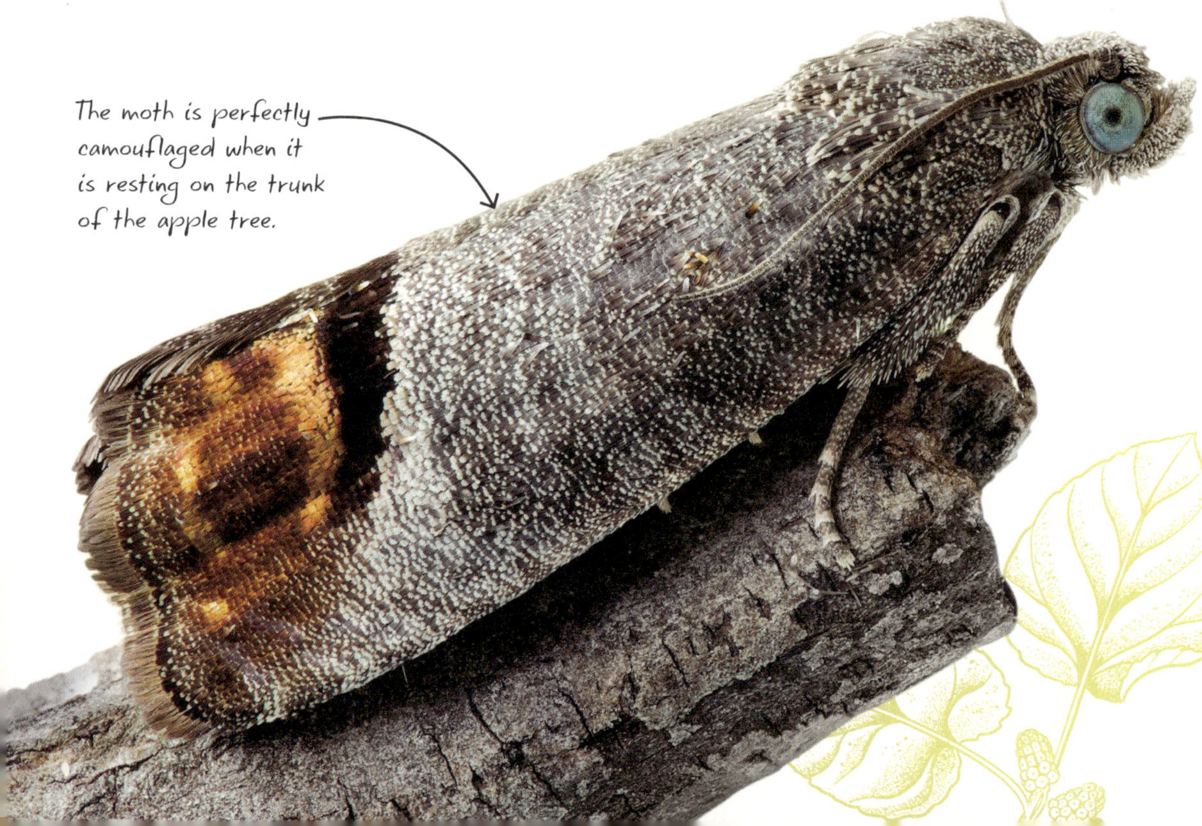

The moth's typical color pattern is pale and mottled, but occasional all-black individuals, called melanic forms, occur.

Up to 2.4 in (60 mm)

Peppered moth

Biston betularia

In the 19th century, throughout many industrial areas, black soot coated the tree trunks where peppered moths rested during the day. The pale mottled ones were visible and were easy prey for birds, but the black varieties remained well-hidden. Soon, only the black moths survived. Then, in the 1950s, new clean-air laws were passed and the amount of soot in the air was reduced. Gradually, the trees were once more covered in lichen, and the original pale moths were better able to survive again.

Notes

· Both pale and black forms of the peppered moth lived in industrial towns and cities— especially in Europe and North America—around 1870–1950

· Twiglike caterpillars feed on the leaves of many different trees and shrubs

Up to 0.9 in (23 mm)

Geranium bronze

Cacyreus marshalli

This pretty, little butterfly was originally only known to live in South Africa. However, in 1978, it was accidentally introduced into southern Europe along with some South African plants. The butterfly was then found in England in 1997, but did not survive. The geranium bronze is now common throughout Spain, Italy, France, and Morocco and has spread farther around the Mediterranean Sea and into Central Europe.

The edges of the wings are checkered.

The broken, pale-and-brown bars across the wings help disguise the butterfly when it rests with its wings closed.

Brimstone
Gonepteryx rhamni

Resting with its wings together, the brimstone butterfly looks just like a pale, dead leaf. It will spend several months hibernating like this over winter, hanging from a twig alongside other "real" leaves. The brimstone is famous for being woken up by warm, winter sunshine and will fly around even if there is snow on the ground. And then it will simply settle back down for several more weeks or months.

Up to 2.9 in (74 mm)

Notes

• Named after brimstone—an old word for the element sulfur, which is also yellow in color

• Makes its home in Europe and Asia

Small, dark blotches just like patches of mold seen in real dead leaves

The wings are drawn out into little leaflike points.

Comma

Polygonia c-album

This butterfly comes in two slightly different colors, depending on when it develops during the year. The first caterpillars to feed in spring become summer butterflies, and they have a rich, golden-brown underside. They lay eggs, and the next generation of butterflies, hatching from chrysalises in the fall, are a much darker brown, almost black. Both forms of butterfly then find hollow trees, rock cavities, or ivy thickets in which to hibernate.

Up to 2.3 in (59 mm)

The irregular wing edges look exactly like a dead and ragged leaf.

The white "c" or "comma" mark looks like a small tear or hole in the leaf.

The spiny caterpillars feed on stinging nettles.

Up to 1.5 in (38 mm)

This moth species has one or two saddle-shaped marks in the middle of each wing, and these arched shapes can help identify it.

Hebrew character

Orthosia gothica

The Hebrew character moth gets its common and scientific names from the distinctive black marks on its front wings. Each mark looks like the letter "nun" in the Hebrew alphabet, or like an ancient Gothic arch on a bridge. This dark blotch is part of a series of wavy patterns on the wings that help the moth blend into its surroundings when it settles to rest.

Up to 1.3 in (32 mm)

The dark-flecked cream borders of the wings look like the toothed edge of a living leaf.

Common emerald

Hemithea aestivaria

Many moths have color patterns of brown, gray, cream, and orange that help them blend into tree trunks or dead leaves, where they hide during the day. The common emerald moth, however, is different—its green color helps it disappear when it settles on a leaf. Green colors are very unusual in adult butterflies and moths.

Peacock

Aglais io

Up to 2.8 in (70 mm)

The peacock butterfly is so named because its eyespots are like those on the display tail feathers of the male peafowl—the peacock. This distinctive butterfly is brightly and strongly colored. Its eyespots are very striking when it rests with its wings out flat, basking in the sunshine. However, when the butterfly closes its wings together, the mottled and streaked underside makes it look just like a dead leaf or piece of broken bark.

Notes

· Males and females at first appear identical, but they do look different when resting in the sunshine

· If you lob a small pebble into the air about 3 ft (1 m) above the butterfly, the territorial male will fly up to investigate, but the female will ignore it

Distinctive blue-and-black eyespots help confuse predators

Up to 1.6 in (40 mm)

The moth gets both its common and scientific names from a white fleck marking shaped like a lowercase "y" or the Greek letter gamma.

Silver Y

Autographa gamma

When they flutter in the long grass, silver Y moths look fragile and awkward, but every year they fly many hundreds of miles northward to make new colonies. They are attracted to lights and can often be found resting on lighted windowsills, or they come in through open windows to settle on walls and ceilings.

Brown-tail

Euproctis chrysorrhoea

When this pure white moth rests with its wings folded over its body, it pokes its deep-brown tail tip up between the wings. Its bristly caterpillars shelter together in a silk web that looks like a handkerchief caught in the branches. It has brittle, hollow hairs containing venom, which break off and can cause skin rashes or red eyes in some people. The caterpillars feed on the leaves of trees and bushes, and they can strip whole hedges of their leaves.

Notes

· In 1782, a major outbreak of the brown-tail moth struck in southern England. The caterpillars destroyed several apple orchards; vast numbers of brown-tail nests were destroyed to try and control the caterpillars

· Today, outbreaks of the moths in Europe and North America can still cause health issues, prompting governments to issue regular warnings

The moth is named after its brown tail tip.

This little brown moth can cause a lot of damage. It prefers the dark to the light and will disappear into clothes if a closet door is opened!

Clothes moths become a problem if closets are not checked very often. After several generations, they can make large holes in fabrics.

Common clothes moth
Tineola bisselliella

The caterpillars of this moth eat clothes and are often blamed for making holes in blankets, carpets, and stored sweaters. The caterpillars spin silk shelters in which to hide, and if lots of these tube-shaped cases are produced together they can form a messy mat. If not dwelling in houses, clothes moths live in animal and bird nests, feeding on feathers and hair. The clothes moth caterpillar eats animal fibers such as wool, silk, and furs—it does not feed on cotton, linen, or synthetic materials, such as nylon or rayon.

Silk moth

Bombyx mori

When the silk moth caterpillar spins a cocoon, liquid silk from glands in the caterpillar's mouth becomes a tough, flexible fiber on contact with air. This silk fiber from the cocoon can later be unwound and collected. Many fibers are wound together and the strands then woven to make the light, soft, but tough fabric for clothes.

Notes

· The silk moth no longer lives in the wild – it is only raised on silk farms

· Silk is difficult to collect and make. This makes it expensive, so it is used only for the most luxurious of clothes

· A silk moth caterpillar is called a silkworm

Each silk cocoon is made of a single strand of silk 1,000–3,000 ft (300–900 m) long.

Taking flight

In a constantly changing world, butterflies and moths are always looking for new patches of food-plant on which to lay their eggs or new areas to make their homes, safely away from predators and parasites. Caterpillars cannot crawl far, so it is up to the winged adults to fly far and wide—spreading out over the countryside.

The painted lady is one of the most widespread butterflies in the world. Each year it migrates hundreds or even thousands of miles.

Migration

After emerging from the chrysalis, many species of butterfly and moth can fly hundreds of miles. These migrations can happen each year, with adults arriving to lay their eggs, and another generation going through the caterpillar and chrysalis stage before continuing the migration onward.

In the spring, monarch butterflies fly north from Central America and spread across North America.

As winter approaches, there is another mass migration south, back to the overwintering sites.

Butterfly wings bend to catch and push air as they flap upward as well as when they flap downward.

Flying styles

Flying is a necessary but dangerous activity. Some butterflies, such as the dogface or peacock, fly fast and straight, while the large white butterfly zigzags around erratically. Both of these methods are good ways to keep predators from catching them in midair. Moths usually fly at night—this helps them avoid birds, but then they have to face bats.

Note

• Many butterflies flap their wings about 5–15 times a second, but the hummingbird hawk moth beats its wings 70–80 times a second—this is just a blur to human eyes

Conservation

Butterflies and moths are more than just pretty insects to admire—they are important parts of the ecosystem and can tell us about the health of the environment. By identifying and counting these insects at a site over many years, scientists can track problems caused by pollution, deforestation, urban development, habitat destruction, and climate change.

Moth traps

Moths are attracted to bright lights. A moth trap allows regular counts and comparisons over years or decades.

Counting butterflies

Butterflies can be counted and mapped regularly across a site—this is called a butterfly transect. Numbers can be compared with previous years to see population changes or the effects of weather.

Apollo butterflies can only survive on cool mountain slopes. If climate change warms these fragile habitats, the butterflies will have nowhere to live.

Endangered species

Falling butterfly numbers can be caused by damage to areas where caterpillar food-plants grow, or to areas where butterflies migrate. Solutions include cutting back or encouraging animal grazing to control shrubs and bushes that shade out food-plants. Dense woodland can be thinned out to allow more light through. Building development can also be controlled to prevent further damage to the countryside.

Extinct, but not forgotten

Butterflies and moths are among the most studied animals in the world. Specimens of species collected hundreds of years ago, even if extinct, can still be examined and compared to modern specimens from other countries or continents. Insect experts, called entomologists, do this to check for changes in genetic makeup and range of color forms and patterns.

The Xerces blue butterfly once lived in sand dunes in the Sunset District of San Francisco, California. Then, houses and offices sprang up in the area. The last Xerces blue was seen flying in 1943, and it is now extinct.

Glossary

alkaloid
Poisonous or bitter-tasting chemical found in plants

androconium
Patch of special scales over a scent-releasing gland on the wings of some male butterflies

antennae
Two long, thin sense organs attached to the head of an insect and containing smell and touch sensors

breed
Mate and then reproduce offspring (young)

butterfly transect
Regular measured walk to count and do checks on butterflies

camouflage
Ability of an animal to blend into its natural surroundings with the help of its colors or patterns

chrysalis
Final form that the caterpillar takes before it turns into an adult butterfly or moth

cocoon
Silk protective cover made by the caterpillar, inside of which it turns into a chrysalis

coremata
Inflatable, tubelike structure in the tail of a male butterfly or moth that produces chemical scents to signal to a female

cultivated
Deliberately grown by humans—in gardens, farmland, or forests

deforestation
Cutting down of forest trees to make way for farmland, roads, or buildings

dimorphism
Having two color forms or patterns, often to show differences in the male and the female; can also be displayed at different times of the year

diversity
Mixture of different plants or animals found at a site

dung
Solid droppings of animals (poop)

ecosystem
Community of plants and animals that live together at a particular place

entomologist
Someone who studies insects

ermine
Soft, white fur of the winter form of stoat; historically, used for fine, expensive clothing

extinct
When all members of an animal or plant species die out and there are none left in the world

food-plant
Type of plant eaten by a particular animal, such as a caterpillar

form
Particular colorway or pattern; a butterfly or moth may have different forms, depending on whether it's male or female, the time of the year, or location around the world

formic acid
Sharp-smelling chemical, a bit like vinegar, produced as a defense by some caterpillars (and ants)

frass
Caterpillar droppings, usually small, dry, hard, oval pellets

glands
Organs inside the body of an animal, such as a caterpillar, that create and release particular chemicals

habitat
Natural home of an animal

hedgerow
Row of shrubs and small trees used as a living barrier in farmland, parks, or gardens

hibernation
Deep sleep or period of inactivity that some animals enter into over winter to hide away and conserve energy

hind wing
One of the two back wings of a butterfly, which has four wings in total

hormone
Chemical produced in animals, including moths and butterflies, that controls growth and other functions

juvenile hormone
Chemical produced in a caterpillar that stops adult features, such as wings and antennae, from growing until it is full-grown and ready to change into a chrysalis

leaf litter
Layer of dead and decaying leaves covering the soil underneath living plants

lek
Gathering of male butterflies or moths (and other animals) where females go to choose a mate

lichen
Small, plantlike growth—a mixture of alga and fungus

microscopic
Something so small that it can only be seen through a microscope

midrib
Central supporting rib, or vein, of a leaf

migration
Deliberate mass movement, usually over large distances, on a yearly or seasonal cycle

mimicry
Looking like something else—colored and shaped to resemble a bird dropping, twig, or another animal

molt
Process of removing tight skin as a caterpillar grows

nectar
Sweet, sugary liquid made by flowers to attract insects

nutrients
Chemicals in food that help an animal or plant to live and grow

overwintering
Hiding or moving elsewhere during winter because it is too wet or cold, or no food-plants are growing

parasite
Animal that lives in or on another animal and gets all its food and shelter from its usually much larger host

phoresy
Gripping onto another animal to get moved

pollination
Movement of pollen, often by insects, from male to female flowers to ensure seed or fruit growth

predator
Animal that kills and eats another animal

prey
Animal that is eaten by another animal

prolegs
Soft, fleshy back legs, up to 16 of them, on a caterpillar, used for holding on to a leaf or twig

pulp
Soft mush

pupa
Another word for the chrysalis stage

reproduction
Process by which an animal produces offspring (young)

scales
Tiny, broad, flat structures that cover butterfly and moth wings and that give them their variety of colors and patterns

segments
Single part of a structure that has repeated units, such as antenna, leg, body

specimen
Single example of a particular species or type

spines
Large, strong, or long hairs developed as prickly defense or sense organs

temperate
Describing a region with mild temperatures

toxins
Poisons, usually those found in poisonous plants or foul-tasting insects

veins
Tubelike structures in leaves and stems that transport nutrients and water; also the tubes in butterfly and moth wings that act as struts to support the wings

venom
Poison injected through fangs or with a sting or inside hollow, stinging hairs of some bristly caterpillars

wingspan
Measurement of the outstretched wings (from tip to tip) of a butterfly or moth

wing tip
Outer tip of each front wing, sometimes differently colored from the rest of the wing, or shaped in a particular way—rounded or sharp

Index

DK Penguin Random House

Senior Editors Marie Greenwood, Kritika Gupta
US Editor Margaret Parrish
US Senior Editor Shannon Beatty
Senior Art Editor Roohi Rais
Project Art Editor Bhagyashree Nayak
Art Editor Nishtha Gupta
DTP Designers Pawan Kumar, Ashok Kumar,
Vijay Kandwal
Senior Picture Researcher Sakshi Saluja
Senior Jacket Designer Rashika Kachroo
Managing Editors Gemma Farr, Roohi Sehgal
Managing Art Editors Elle Ward, Ivy Sengupta
Senior Production Editor Nikoleta Parasaki
Senior Production Controller Inderjit Bhullar
Delhi Creative Head Malavika Talukder
Art Director Mabel Chan

Editorial Consultant Selina Wood

First American Edition, 2025
Published in the United States by DK Publishing,
a division of Penguin Random House LLC
1745 Broadway, 20th Floor, New York, NY 10019

A catalog record for this book
is available from the Library of Congress.
ISBN: 978-0-5939-5931-2

DK books are available at special discounts when
purchased in bulk for sales promotions, premiums,
fund-raising, or educational use. For details, contact:
DK Publishing Special Markets,
1745 Broadway, 20th Floor, New York, NY 10019
SpecialSales@dk.com

Printed and bound in China

www.dk.com

MIX
Paper | Supporting
responsible forestry
FSC™ C018179

This book was made with Forest
Stewardship Council™ certified
paper—one small step in DK's
commitment to a sustainable future.
Learn more at **www.dk.com/uk/
information/sustainability**

The publisher would like to thank the following for their kind permission to reproduce their photographs. (Key: a-above; b-below/bottom; c-center; f-far; l-left; r-right; t-top)

2 SuperStock: Andrey Gudkov / Biosphoto. 3 Dreamstime.com: Oleksii Kriachko (b). 6–127 Dreamstime.com. 6 Alamy Stock Photo: Jörgen Hellberg (cb); Alex Hyde / naturepl.com (cl). Getty Images / iStock: Antagain (cra). 7 Depositphotos Inc: TTstudio (t). 8 Dreamstime.com: John braid / Johnbraid (cl). Shutterstock.com: Stephan Morris (br). 9 Dreamstime.com: Sushil Chikane (br); Jaromir Klein (cl); Filip Fuxa (cra). Getty Images / iStock: mip (tl). 10 Alamy Stock Photo: Andrew Newman Nature Pictures (cr). Dreamstime.com: Matunka (bl). 11 Alamy Stock Photo: Arco / J. Fieber / Imagebroker (b). Getty Images / iStock: Tpopove (tr). 12 Alamy Stock Photo: Darrell Gulin / Danita Delimont (tl); Science Photo Library (bl, br). 13 Alamy Stock Photo: Michael Durham / Minden Pictures (b); Dominic Robinson (clb). Shutterstock.com: Super Prin (t). 15 Alamy Stock Photo: Graham Mulrooney (b). Alamy Stock Photo: The Natural History Museum (t). 17 Dreamstime.com: Yurakp (t). 18 Dreamstime.com: Carlosphotos (t). 19 Dreamstime.com: Simone Brambilla (b). 20 Alamy Stock Photo: imageBROKER.com GmbH & Co. KG / Christian Huetter (b). 21 David Fischer (t). 22 Alamy Stock Photo: Luiz Claudio Marigo / Nature Picture Library (b). 23 naturepl.com: Chi en Lee (t). 24 Dreamstime.com: Oleksii Kriachko (b). 25 Getty Images: Jasius. Getty Images / iStock: phototrip (Stick). 26 Alamy Stock Photo: FLPA (t). 27 Alamy Stock Photo: The Natural History Museum (t). 28 Dreamstime.com: Thawats (b). 29 Science Photo Library: Lawrence Lawry (t). 30 Dreamstime.com: Nexus7 (t). 31 Alamy Stock Photo: Bob Jensen (b). 32 Paul Bertner: (b). 33 Dave Rentz: (t). 34 Dorling Kindersley: Natural History Museum, London (t). 35 Shutterstock.com: Leonardo Mercon (t). 36 Dreamstime.com: Neirfy (t). 37 Alamy Stock Photo: Mark Moffett / Minden Pictures (c). 38 Dreamstime.com: Hakoar (b). 39 Dreamstime.com: David Havel (t). 40 Dreamstime.com: Matthew Omojola (b). 41 Shutterstock.com: Butterfly Hunter (c). 42 Shutterstock.com: Simon Shim (c). 43 Les Catchick: (c). 44 Lorraine Harris. 45 Getty Images: Binu Balakrishnan Photography (b). 46 Getty Images / iStock: PrinPrince (b). 47 Agnès de Pinho: (c). 49 Dreamstime.com: Leerobin (b). 50 Dreamstime.com: Henk Wallays (b). 51 Alamy Stock Photo: Andrew Darrington (t). 52 Getty Images / iStock: Dirk Daniel Mann (b). Shutterstock.com: Svyatoslav A. Knyazev (cr). 53 Alamy Stock Photo: Phil Degginger (bl). Dreamstime.com: Alexander Vysokikh (b). 54 Alamy Stock Photo: Paul R. Sterry / Nature Photographers Ltd (b). 55 Alamy Stock Photo: Alex Hyde / Nature Picture Library (t). 56 Dorling Kindersley: Natural History Museum, London (t). 57 Alamy Stock Photo: Paul R. Sterry / Nature Photographers Ltd (t). 58 Dreamstime.com: Sweety308 (b). 59 Dreamstime.com: Steve Byland (c). 60 Dreamstime.com: Amelia Martin (b). 61 Alamy Stock Photo: Paul R. Sterry / Nature Photographers Ltd (t). 62 Alamy Stock Photo: blickwinkel / Hecker (c). 63 Alamy Stock Photo: Frank Hecker (c). 64 Alamy Stock Photo: DP Wildlife Invertebrates (b). 65 Dreamstime.com: Marcouliana (t). 66 CSIRO: (t). 67 Alamy Stock Photo: Paul Harcourt Davies / Nature Picture Library (t). 68 Alamy Stock Photo: Kjell Sandved (t). 69 Patrick Clement. 70 Alamy Stock Photo: Fotis Panagopoulos (b). 71 Robert Borth. 72 Alamy Stock Photo: Alex Hyde / naturepl.com (b). 74 Depositphotos Inc: Semenovlgor (b). 75 Dreamstime.com: Pimmimemom (b). 76 Dreamstime.com: Mustafa Ozturk (b). 77 Getty Images: Gary Chalker (b). 78 Alamy Stock Photo: blickwinkel / F. Hecker (cl). Dreamstime.com: Samuel Ray (br). 79 Dreamstime.com: Ian Redding (tl); Henk Wallays (b). 80 Dreamstime.com: Spineback (b). 81 Dreamstime.com: David Havel (b). 82 Dorling Kindersley: Natural History Museum, London (b). 83 Alamy Stock Photo: Alex Fieldhouse (c). 84 Janet Graham: (b). 85 Dreamstime.com: Alslutsky (t). 86 Alamy Stock Photo: Selfwood (t). 87 Alamy Stock Photo: Franz Neidl (t). 88 Shutterstock.com: Petr

Muckstein. 89 Dreamstime.com: Cathy Keifer (b). 90 Andrew Bateman: (t). 91 Alamy Stock Photo: Peter Atkinson (t). 93 Dreamstime.com: Stuart Andrews (t). 94 Dreamstime.com: Simon Kovacic (b). 95 Dreamstime.com: Halil Ibrahim Sari (b). 96 Adam Gor: (t). 97 Alamy Stock Photo: Steven Lee Montgomery / Photo Resource Hawaii. 98 Alamy Stock Photo: blickwinkel / F. Hecker (b). 100 Dreamstime.com: Musat Christian (t). 101 Getty Images / iStock: ErikKarits (b). 102 Iain Middlebrook: (b). 103 Alamy Stock Photo: Andrew Newman Nature Pictures (t). 104 Alamy Stock Photo: Andrew Newman Nature Pictures (c). 105 Dreamstime.com: Cosmin Manci (b). 106 naturepl.com: Robert Thompson (t). 107 Getty Images: lukaszprajzner / 500px. 108 Shutterstock.com: Anna Seropiani (b). 109 Alamy Stock Photo: Paul R. Sterry / Nature Photographers Ltd (t). 110 Dreamstime.com: Danut Vieru (b). 111 Alamy Stock Photo: Ross Hoddinott / Nature Picture Library (b). 112 Minden Pictures: Michel Gunther (c). 113 Alamy Stock Photo: Neil Hardwick (t). 114 Dreamstime.com: Cpaulfell (t). 115 Alamy Stock Photo: Arto Hakola (b). 116 SuperStock: Tonci Maletic / Biosphoto (t). 117 Naturfoto www.naturephoto-cz.com: Jiri Bohdal (b). 118 Alamy Stock Photo: blickwinkel / Koenig (t). 119 Alamy Stock Photo: Frank Hecker. 120 Alamy Stock Photo: Terrance Klassen (t). 120–121 Shutterstock.com: Dotted Yeti (b). 121 Alamy Stock Photo: WildScapePhotos (tl). Getty Images / iStock: Nigel Harris (b). 122 Getty Images: Kmatta (bl). Rothamsted Research: (cra). Shutterstock.com: Santi S (b). 123 Dreamstime.com: Thawats (tl). Science Source: Tom McHugh (crb)

DK would like to thank:

Syed Tuba Javed for editorial support; Rituraj Singh for picture research assistance; Polly Goodman for proofreading; Helen Peters for the index; Daniel Long for the feature illustrations; Angela Rizza for the pattern and cover illustrations.

Cover images: *Front:* **Dreamstime.com:** Oleksii Kriachko b; *Back:* **Dreamstime.com:** John braid / Johnbraid cla, Yurakp cra; **Getty Images:** Jasius ca; *Spine:* **Dreamstime.com:** Oleksii Kriachko cb

All other images © Dorling Kindersley Limited